ARUNI KASHYAP

HIS FATHER'S
DISEASE

lubin & kleyner
london

His Father's Disease

First published in 2019 by Context.
This edition published in 2021 by Lubin and Kleyner.

This book is typeset in Trebuchet MS and
Palatino from Linotype GmbH

lubin & kleyner, london
an imprint of flipped eye publishing
www.flippedeye.net

ISBN-13: 978-0-9541570-9-8

LOTTERY FUNDED   Supported using public funding by
ARTS COUNCIL
ENGLAND

HIS FATHER'S DISEASE

ARUNI KASHYAP

CONTENTS

म

SKYLARK GIRL

FROM THIS DISTANCE, the students sounded like birds chirping. They looked carefree, but they had been busy, sprinting across the campus for classes and lectures during the day as well as late into the evening. Often, their clothes were crumpled, and the men had weeklong stubbles. Yet, their eyes were still bright and their young faces glistened in the sunlight. In the evening, a light breeze cooled the campus. Students flocked to the local dhaba or the Chinese takeaway for a quick cup of tea, a snack, a late lunch. The trees on the perimeter of the university's fifty acres were no more than six feet tall, announcing that they were planted less than a year ago, that the university was new and was trying to make its presence felt through conferences such as the one Sanjib was here to attend. Last night, when he arrived, driven by a university-employed driver in a Toyota Innova, it was midnight, but many students were still roaming the grounds. As he took charge of his room at the guesthouse, Sanjib missed his undergraduate days. He couldn't believe that was almost fifteen years ago.

It is around eleven now. He had spent the day attending panels on Indian literature, Dalit literature, literature from Northeast India. And here he was, unable to sleep. The well-lit campus provided no privacy even at night. He found a concrete bench to sit on, right under a tall lamp. They run on solar power, the chief organiser of the conference, a middle-aged man in a black kurta, told them during the Northeast-themed lunch—Naga and Assamese dishes. Sitting on that concrete bench, Sanjib read aloud the story he had selected for his session the next afternoon. It felt odd but he had to read the English translation rather than his own Assamese writing. His English had a thick accent. He halted. How would he tackle questions from the audience? As an undergraduate, he had studied chemistry, but by the time he took his final-year exams, Sanjib had had enough of farty smells in labs. He decided to enrol for a master's programme in Assamese literature. It was a new lease of life: he started writing again, and gathered a loyal list of readers for the poems and stories that were published on the department's wall magazine. By the end of his first year, he had not only made it to several mainstream print magazines but was also elected as the university's magazine editor. It was the most amazing thing that had ever happened to him.

But his mother disagreed. She thought this was the most amazing thing to happen to him—this invitation to read at an international conference. For his mother, Delhi was very far. Delhi meant the army that 'committed atrocities' on the villagers in the Nineties. Delhi was for rich people. Its universities were first class. Delhi was the stepmother who treated the people of Assam poorly. That one of those places in Delhi had recognised her son's calibre and invited him to participate in this all-expenses paid conference was his life's greatest achievement, she felt.

To confirm his participation, he had to email them a draft of one of his stories, translated into English. He cycled six miles in search of a shop with a computer plugged to an internet connection, because even though there were nearly five major mobile phone companies competing for attention with free data and unlimited talk time, none of them worked properly in his village. But first, he requested a friend's mother, a professor in the local college, for help with the translation, but she was too scared to agree. She said that after teaching Keats and Eliot and Shakespeare for twenty-five years in Assamese to students of English honours who didn't understand English, she didn't have the confidence to translate his story into English. This was a big thing, a matter of great prestige for the town, so she would connect him with someone at the Cotton College State University, who would be happy to translate it. The four best stories from the conference would be published in an international anthology, and that may be an incentive for this ambitious young colleague of hers.

Three weeks after he received the letter, Sanjib had travelled to Guwahati, four hours away, with his mother's blessings. During the trip, he wondered who had nominated him for the conference. He had in mind a few possible suspects, but wasn't sure he wanted to think about it. All he had been told was that nomination letters were sought from experts and editors, and that several literary critics had recommended his powerful stories. And now, here he was, sitting on a concrete bench at midnight, practising to read a whole story in a language in which he had never spoken a full sentence.

*

Three weeks before Tejimola's birth, her mother Numoli had eaten so many ripe orange peaches and swallowed so many slippery seeds that she was reminded of her childhood fear. She had strange dreams of becoming a large-trunked tamarind, a lanky and weak papaya, a mango tree where ghosts resided. All night, she twitched on her bed. In the morning, when she told her husband, the wandering businessman Dhaniram Saud, he chided her. He said her fears were baseless. But Numoli disagreed: the dreams were from the morning, and she was facing east then, and she had woken up drenched in sweat. She gave him his cup of tea, made from the dried bark of a mature arjun tree. Aghuni, the tall and large-eyed midwife who would help with the delivery in three weeks' time, was sitting in the backyard. Later, she told Numoli there was nothing to be afraid of. It wasn't a childhood fear that was haunting her; her dreams were anticipating the unborn baby. The lush leafy mango tree that she had transformed into in her dreams, standing all alone in a chrome-yellow harvested paddy field, signalled a healthy baby, she said.

Never before had Aghuni been wrong in her interpretation of dreams, but this time she was. Numoli died giving birth to Tejimola. While cutting the umbilical cord, Aghuni saw tiny, light green buds on Numoli, which confused and scared her so much that she removed them hurriedly. But Numoli was also bleeding and gasping for breath, and Aghuni didn't know what to do to help her. By the time she had bathed the baby, those buds had started to mature into leaves. She plucked them one by one, like plucking fine feathers off the body of a pigeon being prepared for cooking. Soon, Numoli's eyelids were covered with parrot-green peach leaves. Aghuni plucked each one. Bud by bud, leaf by leaf. She scrubbed the baby's skin with powdered lentils only after she had removed all the leaves from the mother's body. Aghuni tried hard to make Numoli look like a normal corpse. She informed Dhaniram Saud about the birth of his daughter. There was no one else in the labour room.

That night, Aghuni told Dhaniram Saud that she would like to stay until the baby girl could take care of herself, and was married off to a good boy who would be able to keep her by working in the rice fields or in the newly founded tea gardens of the British, although those were swarming with workers who spoke a strange language from elsewhere. She loved the baby's dead mother like a sister, she said. Aghuni didn't speak to him of her real fears. She was worried the baby would start sprouting leaves and die, like her mother did. Though she didn't know how she'd prevent it, or how she'd save the girl, Aghuni wanted to linger.

Saud built her a small but strong hut in his backyard. Aghuni had no relatives to return to, so she accepted that hut as her own. But she used it only to keep her clothes and belongings, and the ornaments her mother-in-law had given her on the deathbed. Her days were spent beside the baby's cradle and, later, her bed.

They had named the baby Tejimola but everyone affectionately called her 'Teji'. By the time Saud married a second time, because the village elders pressed him to remarry so that the girl had a mother's caring hands around her, Aghuni had plucked different kinds of leaves off Teji's skin. She used varied pastes, such as that of black-eyed beans or fresh turmeric. She didn't want to repeat her first haphazard, methodless plucking. She thought it was the reason Numoli died, for which she still blamed herself. As a result of Aghuni's regular ministrations, which she masked as 'skin care' so that the stepmother Romola wouldn't know what was going on, Tejimola had the most glowing skin in the whole village. She was dark-skinned, like mature eels and catfishes, and shone even on moonless nights, or at dusk when the day and night met for a while to chat. She also had the most beautiful oval eyes, like slim fishes, with long, thick eyelashes, and only Aghuni worried that they could turn into the vines of a bottle gourd. The worry probably killed her. Two weeks before the red-necked leaf-green parrot sang to a middle-aged Saud, who was packing his bags for a trip around the world to sell his wonderful handicrafts and silk clothes, Aghuni passed away in her sleep.

The parrot sang:

When you see me, you frown,
Into a lady your daughter has grown,

When will you get her

a groom from the town?

Its shrill voice and accusatory tone reminded Saud of his
second wife, Romola, who was the most quarrelsome woman
in the village and treated Tejimola like a slave. He looked at
the bird, sighed and assured him that, as soon as the steamer
reached the chest of the Brahmaputra river, he would begin
the search for a handsome groom for his only daughter.

As was the case whenever Saud travelled, the night his
boat floated towards the Bay of Bengal, Romola cooked
delicious dishes for her three sons but gave Teji only leftover
rice with salt, made her sleep on the floor on a bamboo mat
and forced her to do the dishes, wash clothes and even tether
the cows when they returned home, a man's job.

Tejimola was not saddened by this, for she loved the only
person she could call 'Ma'. The night Saud left, a small green
bud sprouted on her finger. She used sandalwood paste to
remove it as soon as she could. Teji had loved Aghuni and
she missed her.

*

Sanjib had never thought himself a handsome man. During
those postgraduate days in Gauhati University, it was Riti
who made him feel that way. She had accosted him after
an open-mike on campus and asked if he would share his
mobile number and go out for coffee with her. When he said
he didn't like coffee, she called him every day for weeks
inviting him to have tea, Thumbs Up, CocaCola, Citra, cane
juice, until he agreed. 'Tea', he said. 'I will have tea with
you.' During what they would later call their first date, he
was surprised that someone so attractive and interesting
was drawn to him. They dated for two years, and everything
seemed just right during those years. But he knew he had

made a mistake when she took him home for the first time — a huge two-level building in one of the most expensive parts of the city. Their living room had an artificial stream and an aquarium that covered the length of the wall and the tables had expensive wooden and bronze statues. The marble floor was so clean that he felt his cheap 200-rupee chappals were permanently tainting it.

Later he told her, you know there is no future to this relationship. Don't you know my father is a farmer? He doesn't even own land. Some years, he doesn't get to sharecrop because the Bangladeshi immigrants do it at cheaper rates. And your parents own one of the largest construction companies in Northeast India. Must every relationship have a future, she had asked, voice quivering. He paused. They were sitting on a wooden bench in the university campus. It was April. Final exams were at least a month away. She was planning to go abroad for her doctoral studies. Or M. Phil. He didn't know. She had never discussed it with him. The krishnachura tree was in full bloom, its flowers reaching towards the blue spring skies like flames feeding on a large heap of straw. He asked, what is the point then? I don't want to be anyone's 'timepass'. Later, she had texted him, he was never timepass; what a horrible way to brand their relationship. There was meaning in it. And unlike him, she saw a future for them. He read her text. He thought about the marble floor and his tattered chappals that were stitched and repaired by the village cobbler. He replied that she was able to see that future because she was on higher ground. He still had a lot to build. A ladder, a staircase — god knows what else — to reach her level. The marble floor and those tattered slippers. Such a mismatch.

At the conference luncheon — where the panellists were supposed to meet and bond with the moderator and plan the discussion — he felt like a misfit. The food laid on the table was colourful and looked delicious and fresh, with a lot of crunchy vegetables, but he didn't know what to pick. The labels didn't mean anything to him: paella, tortillas, fajitas, quesadilla, guacamole. For a second, he wanted to fish out his phone to Google those words, but he was shy. They said lunch was going to be Mexican and he was looking forward to it, but he didn't know the names would be in Spanish, too. He filled his plates with rice, beans and vegetables though he knew it was not quite right—something should be mixed with something, and he was doing it all wrong. Embarrassed, he sat in one corner. The rest of the panellists joined him after reading his nametag. Their hellos were cheerful enough but he was relieved to meet John, the Naga writer. John knew Nagamese, and Sanjib spoke it fluently. Sanjib hoped he could be friends with John and hang around him. For a moment, he forgot his regret at having accepted the invitation. What would happen if his story were accepted in some journal that he had never seen? He didn't know. He was a schoolteacher who didn't even get his salary regularly.

He felt he was back in Riti's house—a large aquarium, marble floors, his tattered slippers. The moderator was a tall, well-built Punjabi man who introduced himself as an editor. He said his publishing house took a lot of pride in publishing writers from the Northeast. Most of the writers present there, the Arunachali man, the Mizo woman, the Khasi girl and the Nepali writer from Sikkim, seemed to know the editor already. They laughed like long-time friends and occasionally referred to other writing conferences they had been to together. Sanjib realised he was the only one among them who didn't write in English. He felt like he shouldn't be there; like that classmate who came to school with long nails and smelly clothes and got bullied by everyone. So, he tried to focus on his food instead. The rice was lime flavoured. The vegetables were crunchy. The green paste was amazing.

The editor said they must show the world what a real Northeastern story was. I am like a crusader for stories from the Northeast, he told Sanjib. So nice to meet you, young man. I am really looking forward to your reading and finally finding out what you have written, he added Sanjib thanked him but was also surprised that the editor hadn't read his story yet. He would be the one nominating stories for the international anthology, John had said.

What's his name, Sanjib asked.

John was surprised. He raised his voice, 'Toi na jani?'

Sanjib said he didn't. Impress him, John whispered, stabbing a piece of chicken with his fork. If you impress him, you may even get a book contract.

I see, Sanjib responded, and thought about his mother. How proud she would be.

*

Tejimola was surprised at her stepmother's generosity. She had asked for a good cotton dress from her dead mother's shelf to wear to her best friend's wedding. Instead, Romola brought out an expensive golden muga-silk dress from Sualkuchi. Tejimola hesitated. But Romola smiled warmly and said, 'Ah, you don't have to wear those old designs. And you should start wearing a full-sleeved jakit-blouse too. That is one convenient thing the British people brought with them—instead of wrapping the reeha, now you can wear a blouse under your dress. Here, I have a matching blouse too.'

Tejimola hesitated still. 'Ma, are you sure?'

'Ah, I am growing old, my dear Teji! If the grown-up girl of the house doesn't wear my clothes, who will? Haven't you seen your brothers? God knows what kind of women they will bring home when they grow up. If this old lady gets a corner to rest in and two meals a day after they bring home women to share their beds, I will consider it enough. But then, who would wear my beautiful clothes? You must deck up for your best friend's wedding. Will you be able to go alone?'

'Yes, I can go alone.' She looked at the mekhela-sador hesitantly and added, 'It is a beautiful set.'

But Romola had plans. Sinister plans. While packing the dress in a jute satchel, she had placed a smouldering wood and a small brown-skinned rat in the folds.

The path to Tejimola's best friend's house was windy. It was the month of Phagun and blood-red silk cotton flowers spread a carpet on the road. The long, slim petals looked like a sex worker's nails. Teji felt something moving in her jute satchel. She wanted to open it and check. But she was scared because her stepmother had warned her not to look inside before reaching the wedding. Romola had said that the clothes would become dirty because it was so windy and dusty. She knew her mother's anger. Teji had been overwhelmed at the sudden display of love, and didn't want to disappoint her. She walked faster, resolving to check what was wrong only after reaching her friend's place, where she would take a bath and change. She didn't see the occasional wisps of smoke coming from the jute satchel because she had tucked it between her arms and pressed it to her body.

When she finally unwrapped the dress, Teji was horrified at seeing it partially burnt and rat-chewed. She sat in a corner of the changing room and wept. Her mother would kill her. The dress was a wedding gift from an old aunt.

Sokhi, her best friend, tried to console her, 'Come on, Teji, you are not responsible for this.'

'But how do I explain it, Sokhi?'

'You don't have to explain anything—just tell her the truth.'

Someone called out to Sokhi from the other room. It was time she bathed. The smell of flowers and different kinds of lentil paste that would be applied on her body during the ritual bath dispersed the sullenness of the room. Sokhi opened a wooden box and took out a new pat-silk set that she had received as a gift and gave it to Tejimola. But Teji couldn't enjoy the wedding. A fear pulled at the tender strings of her heart like the sorrowful tone of a buffalo-horn aerophone. The teller of wonderful stories, her best friend, with whom she had shared the news of her first period and first loves, was going away. She wondered when they would meet again, and hoped to marry someone who lived in her best friend's new village. But the fears didn't subside; like monsoon rivers, they overflowed, since she did not have answers about the burnt silk dress. When the women sang the parting song, and Sokhi went to hug each person she was close to, Teji couldn't stop crying.

O Lucky Daughter of the house!
With betel nuts in your hands,
Go say goodbye to your mother.

With silk clothes in your hands,
Go touch the feet of your father.
With worn-out toys in your hands,
Go kiss the forehead of your little brother
With gold ornaments in your hands,
Go clasp the palms of your elder brother.

With mischief twinkling in your eyes,
Go hug your closest girlfriends,
Whom you will never meet again—
Remember: a girl's life is just a
String of ephemeral images
formed by meeting nimbus clouds.

Before leaving the courtyard of this house,
at least turn back once, if you
don't want the pots and pans of this house
to follow you down the dusty road.

O Lucky Daughter of the house!
O Lucky Daughter of the house!

Teji's mother didn't believe her. She caught hold of Teji by her long, silky hair and slapped her. As punishment, she put the girl to grinding rice. Tejimola pleaded, said that she would do all her mother wanted, but Romola must trust her. But Romola had planned Tejimola's death for a long time, and this was a golden opportunity. Saud wasn't around. At first, she smashed the girl's right hand with the grinder. When she cried, 'Ma, you gnashed my right hand,' Romola said, 'Use your left.' And then her feet. When she cried, 'Ma, you smashed both my feet, please let me go,' Romola asked her to use her head. She cracked her skull too, with the stave.

Romola buried Tejimola in the backyard. All these years, her flesh and blood had been waiting. As soon as Romola turned her back, the girl's flesh started to germinate and gradually turned into a gourd-bearing creeper. The soil sucked up her blood, drawing nourishment. The leaves, twigs and the roots protected her soul, kept it intact.

In the lonely backyard, during windy afternoons, the plant sang songs, and the fresh smell of gourds would spread. It was normal for songs to float in the slow, windy afternoons thickened by the sounds of cooing doves. The creeper's songs were soft. Anyone near enough to hear it would believe a woman was singing someplace faraway.

*

The auditorium was massive. Even though there were at least a hundred people there, it looked like the event was poorly attended.

Sanjib saw no familiar faces. John met someone from Calcutta, an old friend who had come for the panel. The moderator said he would be back after a visit to the campus's smoking zone. Sanjib looked around. Everyone's clothes fit so nicely, he noticed, only his were ill-fitting. He was also surprised how male students turned up in shorts and three-quarters and sleeveless vests. How carelessly the women wore their cotton saris—as if they were in bed until a moment ago—and yet how good they looked in them. He found a corner for himself and returned to the printed pages he would read soon. On the margins, he had written down the pronunciation of some English words in Assamese letters. He had practised reading the story with the translator. She had a posh accent—the kind of accent Riti had, the kind he would never be able to acquire. She had gone to an English-medium school that allowed them to wear skirts, unlike his Assamese-medium school where the girls had to wear green-bordered mekhela sador and the boys had to wear khaki pants. For a long time, that khaki pair was the only one he had. He kept it well, and during festivals and weddings, sprinkled water on it and used a steel bowl filled with hot water to iron it. One day, when he told Riti that those were the only tailored pants he possessed until he moved to Guwahati to study chemistry, she had blinked and said that it sounded like a fable. He said nothing. Later, when they broke up, he imagined her standing in front of him and said, there is nothing fabulous about it. It is how things are for many people. And it is my reality, too.

The moderator smelled good. He was wearing some cologne that was mild and powdery. So, what is your story about, he asked Sanjib. They were waiting for the rest of the panellists to arrive. Sanjib still couldn't get over the fact that the moderator hadn't read his story.

It is a folktale retold. Set during colonial times.

The moderator was excited. So you are looking at the exploitation of your state from the colonial period?

No, not at all. It is just a popular story. I am just retelling it with some more twists and turns.

The moderator's eyebrows creased and he looked disappointed. Why is it so popular?

Because the character, who is repeatedly killed by her stepmother, refuses to give up on life. You know, people find it inspiring. We have, after all, refused to give up on living, despite all the violence. The Eighties and Nineties were so horrible. Sanjib spoke slowly, in Hindi, which was better than his English. But he was annoyed that the moderator continued to ask him questions in English.

John hadn't returned yet. A young student from the organising committee was checking the microphone. Another student stood next to her with bouquets.

Why hide behind a folktale, Sanjib? You should write about those things that you just mentioned—the violence, human rights abuse, those are the real issues. That is where the real story from your region is; it is the kind of story that makes news and gets people sit up and notice.

Sanjib was puzzled, not because every time the moderator used the word 'real' his voice became louder and more impatient, but because Sanjib didn't understand what he meant by a real story. He just said, I am not hiding behind a folktale. There is a reason why people retell this story over and over—many contemporary writers have retold it, actually. It is because we find inspiration in the girl who refuses to die. And we are relieved that the stepmother is finally brought to justice. In reality, that doesn't happen. Delhi and its representatives are never made responsible.

Interesting, the moderator said, nodding, and asked, then why should people outside your state read this story?

I don't know. I never said they should or shouldn't. I wrote it in Assamese—the reader in Delhi never figured during the composition process.

Sanjib got a long, cold stare, and he thought, I am never making it to that coveted anthology.

Maybe because of the guilt, for weeks, Romola didn't go to where Tejimola lay buried. So, one afternoon, after lunch, when an emaciated beggarwoman came asking for gourds, she was surprised.

'Foolish beggar, you must be daydreaming. I haven't had a gourd in weeks and, in fact, to cook the rohu fish for dinner, I just sent my son to look for a good mature one in someone's house. Where the hell have you seen gourds?'

'I wouldn't lie, Aaideu,' the woman exclaimed. 'You are the owner of this house; if you don't want to give me a gourd when you have so many, I have nothing to say.' The beggarwoman turned to leave.

'I really don't know what you are talking about. If you have seen any, go help yourself. I have no problem,' Romola said and continued working her foot loom, trying to make a beautiful blue flower bloom. Irritated, she muttered about greedy beggar women.

Soon after, howling and crying, the woman came running and fainted right in front of her. Romola was stunned. Grumbling, she rushed indoors and returned with a glass of cold water that she sprinkled on the woman's eyes and face.

'Are you okay? Are you okay? What happened? What did you see?' When she regained consciousness, she sat up, sweat still dripping from her head, beads of perspiration still emerging on her forehead. 'There is a ghost in that creeper plant! It says it is Tejimola and her stepmother killed her because of a silk dress! Who is she?'

Romola paced in the veranda. She was petrified because some people in the village were asking, and she had said that Teji never returned from her best friend's wedding. Bracing herself, Romola decided to do something about the situation—it's just a plant, Tejimola is dead! Romola took a huge machete and went to the backyard. She strained her ears and heard a parting song, sung at weddings, coming as if from a distance. Without wasting any more time, she chopped the plant to pieces. The seeds of the gourd plant flew around, its juice stained her white dress, and she panted and sweated. There were four hundred and fifty-nine large gourds in the plant, ninety-two immature ones, and three thousand and forty-five flowers, which she picked up one by one, first on her own and later helped by her two sons who returned from the fields after their tang-guti games. The eldest, who had gone looking for a gourd, hadn't returned yet. Together, they dug a deep hole in the farthest corner of the garden and buried the rest of the plant.

This time, in that farthest corner, there grew a plant of reddish elephant lime. A few weeks later, when the yet-tobe-men village cowherds came asking for the ripe limes on a lush plant growing in the farthest corner of her backyard garden, Romola told them to help themselves. She didn't think about it further until they began screaming at the top of their voices and fleeing.

She was sitting in her courtyard, grating a coconut. One of the boys flung himself on the ground in front of her, foaming at the mouth. Another one sat and cried like a baby. Before fainting, this second boy told her about a singing lime tree:

Don't you dare stretch your hands,

I am not a lime tree,

ground and buried

because of a silk dress,

it's me,

it's me,

Tejimola.

*

John's tale, set in New York and Kohima, was a love story between an Indian man and an American woman who visits Nagaland. The Mizo writer's story starts on the day when the state of Mizoram was bombarded by the Indian Air Force. The main character, a young girl displaced during the bombardment, is looking for her parents, and during her search, the writer provides a cinematic look at the ravaged portions of the city. The Khasi author's story was set in Bangalore and Shillong, about a man who has an affair with an injured Naga woman insurgent while his Bengali wife takes care of his family in Bangalore.

Sanjib was deeply impressed by most of the stories, but he liked the Mizo writer's story best. He couldn't stop thinking about the young girl, because it reminded him of his elder sister and mother, who had to flee their home when the soldiers had surrounded their village and started burning houses to fish out insurgents. He wasn't even born then. Sanjib also liked the Khasi author's story about the man's infidelity, and wanted to read the story again to learn how to arrive at a language so intimate and descriptions so impartial that he didn't judge the man but felt sorry for all the characters torn apart by their desires. He didn't connect to John's story at all. He couldn't understand the point of bringing the American woman to Nagaland when they could have had that fight in New York as well. Nagaland was like a curtain; the characters didn't even eat Naga food in the story. They kept eating chow mein. But when John asked him if he liked it, he said it was excellent. When Sanjib read, the moderator walked out for four minutes during his ten-minute long reading. He felt insulted and it affected the way he read, but tried not to think about it. Sanjib wondered if the moderator was dealing with an emergency at home. He tried to forgive him and continued reading. At the end of the reading and discussion, a question-and-answer session started.

A young woman from the audience asked the first question. She introduced herself at length, but Sanjib didn't get the name or her profession. Perhaps it was her accent. She spoke with a lisp that made her sound sexy, but because he wasn't used to people talking that way, he found it difficult to follow most of what she said. She started by appreciating the panellists for their thoughtful conversations and also the university for organising the conference and he wondered why she couldn't come to the point. Sanjib did manage to catch that she was writing her doctoral thesis on literature from Northeast India, but he didn't get the name of the university she was associated with. She sounded intelligent, he thought. She said her question was for Sanjib: why had he decided to write about this magical world, instead of the insurgencies, the violence and the more immediate, the more topical stories. He was surprised by the question. Back home, his Assamese readers did not expect him to write about this or that topic. He was free to write anything. When she ended, the moderator said 'good question' and a lot of people clapped, as if the woman was calling out Sanjib for doing something terrible. Sanjib paused, and wondered how the moderator could comment on the quality of the question when he wasn't present for much of the reading. Sanjib asked the young woman to repeat her question. There was an awkward silence before she responded to his request.

This is funny, Sanjib started to answer, in his halting English, peppered with Hindi sentences, and because his Hindi was also thickly accented, he didn't sound serious. It seemed as if he was joking or making fun of the girl. But he wasn't. This is funny, Sanjib said, because no one in Assam would ask me that question—why don't you write about the violence? The woman was in the front row, standing, with the microphone close to her lips and a smile on her face. When he said 'this is funny', her smile vanished in an instant. As if he said something hurtful and completely unexpected. But he continued, in fact, this story has been translated because people thought it was a good break from the violence when it was conceived and published in Assamese. We read about violence and gun battles and rapes and dismembered bodies every day in the papers. So people in Assam wouldn't mind reading this story. There is no burden of expectations on me when I write in Assamese. So I really don't know how to answer your question. The questioner thanked him, coldly, without the enthusiasm and warmth the question had. Sanjib wondered if she thought she had asked an excellent question and was disappointed he didn't reward that brilliance with an answer that acknowledged its quality. He wanted to get out of there soon. And return home. The stories written by his co-panellists had humbled him, and that was all that mattered to him.

Gulab jamuns and samosas were served outside the auditorium. Sanjib was hungry. The other panellists were talking to the moderator, signing books, or talking to the students. He didn't want to talk to anyone. Sanjib checked his cellphone for the time—the cab would come in a couple of hours and take him to the airport.

Excuse me, can I say something? It was the woman who asked him that question. She seemed upset still and her voice was quivering. She paused a little, creases forming on her forehead, as if she was about to say something unpleasant that she didn't want to articulate, but had to because it would be the right thing to do. Sanjib smiled at her, but he was still thinking about the moderator who hadn't heard his story in its entirety, about the people who clapped when the woman who claimed to be a scholar on literature from India's Northeast asked him that question. Why had they clapped, what was so right about her question that people had begun clapping even before he spoke? And why didn't they clap when he finished answering.

Yes, please?

I don't know how to say this, but I think it is important for me to express it.

Oh sure, Sanjib tried to be encouraging.

I just wanted to say that I didn't appreciate your answer. I just felt so attacked—I just felt—I mean, I love literature from Northeast, but don't know why you got so defensive.

Sanjib was shocked. I wasn't attacking you. I was just telling you how things are back home. I was merely answering your question.

The woman became a bit more impatient. She asked him a question that further surprised him: do you think I asked you a question that I shouldn't have asked?

Sanjib shook his head. Not at all, you have every right to ask any question you want, but I just found it very amusing, and I wasn't insulting you. You know what is even funnier? Even when we write about violence, we are asked to be quiet and discreet. Write about violence, but don't name anyone. The non-threatening Northeastern who writes about real and topical issues is what everyone wants, and that's the one who is always garlanded with prizes and fellowships. And researchers like you base your doctoral research papers on their work. Do you have anything to say about that? I think the problem is that people only look at things in binaries. No one here knows that I have written several stories about the violence committed by the armies in the Eighties and Nineties.

There was an awkward silence. The woman did not appear mollified.

I am sorry, I have to leave. Perhaps this was a mistake, she said quickly, and rushed away.

Sanjib stood there, watching her back and her ponytail, vanish into the crowd. He wasn't sure what he did wrong, why she was offended, why she felt attacked just because he disagreed with her.

He felt a pat on his back. It was the moderator. You did well, he said, like an uncle who wants to be the cool uncle when the parents are angry with a child. Your story got some good questions; you did well, the moderator repeated.

Sanjib turned to him and replied, but you didn't listen to my story. You weren't even there for the first four minutes.

*

By the time Dhaniram Saud reached his village, it was autumn. In Lower Assam, he had met a guy who he thought would be the best for Tejimola. Hardworking and muscular, he touched the feet of elders, listened to his mother, helped his grandmother grind her betel with limestone until it was bright red and sharp on the tongue. He wasn't a smoker. He slept early, rose early. His skin was the colour of gold for he always bathed before sunrise. As the boat approached the village, the boatman's song almost sent him into a thin lull:

Kanai, take us to the other shore,

The sun has created long shadows now.

If you take too long to reach home,

Your milk will curdle,

Won't your mother scold you then?

Won't your mother scold you then?

Kanai, take us to the other shore,

Otherwise your milk will curdle!

As soon as you can!

The excited chatter of one of his crewmembers woke him up.

'Look at that!'

'No, no, I have seen many, but this is divine.'

'Arrey, don't go, it might be charmed …'

'Yes, yes, we are not very far from Mayong—the land of sorcerers!'

'That's true; they turn human beings into buffaloes and make them work in the fields.'

Dhaniram Saud sat up, wore his turban, checked if the tail fell gracefully on his spine and walked out from his resting place, where a soft bed was spread for him with fruits, water and betel nuts placed beside it in a finely woven creel. A most wonderful sight awaited him: he had never seen a bigger, brighter, redder lotus in all his life, as large as an umbrella crafted from bamboo. In the distance, he saw the large steamers of the British companies moving slowly towards Calcutta, carrying goods and students who went to study in colleges there. 'I am going to pluck this for Tejimola, only a daughter like her, only a beautiful girl like her deserves it.'

The lotus sang, retelling a mournful story, starting with a rat and a tiny, smouldering piece of wood. Dhaniram Saud didn't believe her, but suddenly, when they were about to uproot the misleading, evil lotus, he said, 'Stop!'

He looked closely at the blood-red flower and opened both his palms.

He placed a fresh piece of betel on one, and spat out chewed betel on the other. 'If you are the real Tejimola, you will turn into a skylark and come and peck on the chewed betel on my right palm. If you are some ghost trying to delude me, you will come and chew the fresh piece of betel on my left palm. If I have lived a virtuous life, if I have respected my parents, if I truly believe in God, you will be compelled by the divine forces of nature to follow my command!'

The air was still.

A bee went near the lotus but did not sit on it.

A dragonfly flew to the centre of it but seemed to change its mind.

The steamer carrying goods and students to Calcutta was far away now. It looked like it was merging into the hills.

One man in the crew said, 'The lotus breathes, I felt it.'

'I command you. If I have lived a virtuous life, if I have respected my parents, if I truly believe in God ...' Saud screamed again.

When he reached home that afternoon, he carried a caged brown skylark.

The stepmother didn't ask about it. When asked where Tejimola was, she began howling and said that his daughter had eloped with a man when she went to her best friend's wedding. So ashamed was Romola that she hadn't told the villagers. Her three sons, in varying stages of adolescence with varying lengths of incipient beards on their chins and upper lips, lied that they went to enquire in her best friend's village and several people confessed secretly, saying that they didn't want to taint the name of the famous Dhaniram Saud.

He took a long piece of red-bordered sador, walked up to the cage and said, 'My daughter, now I command you to take your real form and wear this.'

ব

BIZI COLONY

(1)

LONG BEFORE MY younger brother Bablu began telling our neighbours that Ma sucked Papa's best friend Hriday Uncle's dick while Papa was away on official tours to New Delhi, he would touch the breasts of our forty-year-old maid and ask her how it felt. When the timid Geeta-baideo wept, saying that she was the one who brought him up, washed his ass after he crapped as a baby, he beat her up with a cane. Bablu was around twelve. That evening, when Papa returned from work, he asked a sullen Geeta what had happened. She didn't say anything because she wanted to protect Bablu. Ma hesitantly told him bits and pieces of what had taken place. Papa beat up Bablu with whatever he could lay his hands on.

Back when Bablu was around nine, he broke the skull of a daily wager who came to weed our garden because the man said that Bablu was crazy and muttered nonsense.

Ma complained to Papa that evening, 'Do you even care about what's going on here?'

Papa had had a long day at work. Tired and annoyed, he asked Ma, 'Are you his stepmother?' He accused her of loving her younger son less. 'You complain about your younger son all the time, like a stepmother! As if the elder one is a saint?'

Bablu pointed his finger at Ma. 'You are a stepmother.' He was young then. So young that he hadn't started calling Ma a 'bitch' and a 'slut'.

Ma cried all night. She screamed at Papa: how could you say that, how could you even think like that, how was she to deal with all this nonsense all day when he was two hours away by bus, sitting in his air-conditioned office where he had a sassy personal assistant to bring him tea. She used the word 'rosoki' actually, not 'sassy', and that irked Papa even more. Angered, he caned Bablu the next morning. Since Bablu was only nine years old then, Papa could hold him upside down by his legs. As he beat Bablu in a rage, Papa demanded to know if he would trouble Ma anymore. A petrified Ma called to our neighbours for help. They rebuked Papa. One shouldn't 'overdo' things, they said. It was truly sad, they said, to see Ma arguing with a whole band of Bangladeshi workers, who had arrived with their gang to corner her about the daily wager's injury. When she gave them money, they left without another word. Geeta-baideo said that that's what 'these Bangladeshis' wanted. Each and every person nodded, lips twisted with distaste. As if they had smelt fart—like the smell that came from the chemistry lab of the school nearby.

Papa sat down on a sofa, his head bowed. Ma went up to him and ran her fingers through his thick hair. She asked why he could not control his anger.

From the other room, Bablu roared. He said, when he grew up, he would kill Papa.

Our neighbours went in. They told him sweetly that he shouldn't say such things, only bad boys uttered such things, are you a bad boy? He said he wasn't a bad boy, but now he wanted to be one because he wanted to stab Papa. When the kind-hearted, free advice-dispensing neighbours repeated their counsel, Bablu asked them to get lost. Papa made a swift move towards the room, cane in hand.

(2)

Bablu started to steal quite early. The second time he stole money, my cousin Junmoni was visiting. Junmoni had tried to take his seventh standard finals three times, in vain. So my uncle wanted him to spend some days with Ma and Papa in a 'studious atmosphere'. Ma warned him that there was no such atmosphere, that her younger son was very unruly, fought with everyone who visited. But Uncle insisted. In the middle of the night, I sensed someone entering my room. I had left my door open because our cat Munu hadn't returned when I had gone to bed. He liked to sit on my table, watching me with half-shut eyes, purring loudly. If I slept with the door latched, he woke everyone up by meowing incessantly in front of my door until I opened it. So, when I heard soft sounds, I didn't bother to switch on the light. But the next morning, my wallet was empty. My hundred-rupee notes, four of them, were missing. When I told Papa that all my money was gone, he questioned Bablu. Ma began crying. She said it would be so embarrassing if Junmoni told everyone in her hometown about this. Junmoni kept assuring her that he wasn't much of a talker. When Bablu continued to deny that he'd taken the money, Papa started to thrash him. Bablu howled, saying that he would never do such a thing. But Ma kept quiet, held him in her arms, and said, don't cry, don't cry, don't cry.

When the pandemonium subsided—except for Bablu who continued to hurl abuses at Papa—Junmoni said he was too scared to stay on any longer and would go to Shillong with his friends before leaving for home. He returned late that night. The next morning, he showed us the hundred rupee digital watch he had bought, the cheap green shades he must have picked up for a hundred-fifty from the kiosk at the bus stand, and a red T-shirt probably bought from the footpath vendor. I showed no interest. Ma looked hard at Junmoni and said, 'Your father loves you so much, gives you money whenever you want, why won't you study well?'

He said he would return home and study well, because he wanted to go to Mumbai to learn acting and become a star. 'I am already learning breakdance,' he said and showed us a few steps, moving his head to the right, to the left.

No one was interested in discussing the topic, except Bablu. He asked Junmoni a thousand questions. (How to go to Bombay? How to pursue a career as an underworld don? Which train must one take?) until Junmoni was so tired that he snapped at Bablu, 'STOPASKINGMETHESAMETHINGS.' Bablu hit him with a broom. Papa walked out of his study, Bablu ran out of the house, leaving a howling Junmoni sprawled on the floor. Junmoni left the next morning. In the evening, my uncle called. Papa picked up the phone, heard him out and said, 'She is your sister, why would I scold her? You should scold her.' He handed the phone to Ma. At the end of what was evidently a monologue, Ma looked up at us and said, 'Who gave money to Junmoni? I didn't. He is drunk on moonshine and my brother is inconsolable! Gosh, what is happening to the youth of this country?'

That night, Ma slept in Bablu's bed and wept a lot. Papa looked distressed and paced the veranda. 'Am I a failed father? Why do I get so angry?' he whispered.

(3)

I had to tell Niyor about Bablu because I couldn't sleep the night before. I went to the kitchen in search of a sharp knife several times, but the thought of plunging it into my heart or stomach was so scary that I gave up the plan. I also fished out one of my 7 O'Clock blades (Super Stainless) from the black shaving kit and trailed it over the blue veins of my wrists over and over, never quite making contact with skin. In the other room, Papa and Ma were crying. From Bablu's room, the stench of shit. I wondered how the others were managing. How the others were breathing. I stayed awake, trying to study for the economics test.

We were returning from school in a crowded bus. It was evening. I told Niyor that I couldn't sleep at night. He said that meant I would pass the test with flying colours. I said that I wasn't awake studying for the test; we were at the police station until midnight because Bablu had been someplace fourteen-year-olds weren't supposed to be. When I told him exactly where, he didn't understand how serious the situation was. Then I gave him a description of the cowdungy gunny bags, and the blue plastic sheets that people covered themselves with when they slept, the smell of burnt marijuana leaves, the men in stained buttonless shirts staring at my mother, and the way she had covered her head with her sador. Niyor stopped speaking. I didn't tell him about the man who stood in front of Ma with his dick hanging out of his unzipped trousers like a banana. I didn't tell him that the police officer looked at Papa and said, 'Avoid'—a monosyllabic word of caution, to avoid attention from the man with the unzipped trousers who was probably trying to provoke us into a fight.

The crowded bus was so noisy, mostly full of people returning from their offices, and yet it felt to me that the world had come to a standstill—because that was the first time I told anyone about Bablu. In a crowded bus. Full of tired people. Sweaty. Stuffy. In a crowded bus, I had finally spoken about Bablu. To Niyor, my best friend.

After a long time, he asked me, if Bablu was the reason I never invited him to my house, and I said yes. But I wanted him to ask me more. I didn't want to tell him that Bablu says Ma sucked Hriday Uncle's cock. But I wanted to tell him about the things I had avoided that day, following the police officer's instructions. The drug peddlers I had seen and avoided. Ma held my hand firmly, as if we were on a tightrope. I wanted to tell him that I saw sex workers for the first time and avoided their gaze; their garish makeup, gaudy, revealing dresses, deep cleavages. There were also men who wore lipstick and eyeliner, and gem-studded bangles flashed on their wrists. I wanted to tell him how, earlier, we had waited until eleven at night for Bablu to return. How none of his classmates knew where he was because he hadn't been to school. But Bablu had left home in the morning carrying his blue lunch box and school bag, wearing the grey school trousers, with Ma prompting him from the veranda to walk faster because he might miss the school bus.

In Bizi Colony, at around 1 a.m., when our shoes were caked with drying black scum and stomachs so filled with the smells of the neighbourhood that we might throw up on each other, we found Bablu. He was lying in a ditch. Actually, it was the police officer with the horrible breath who found him. How could Ma hug Bablu even though his clothes smelled so horrible? When he was brought home—released by the police officer without pressing charges because he was young and Ma was a professor—Geeta-baideo, who had been waiting for us, immediately threw up on the living-room floor because she had just finished dinner. We had all gone because Ma didn't want Papa to go alone, and I wanted to accompany Ma.

In the crowded bus, I told Niyor that, last night, when I couldn't sleep, I'd looked around for the room freshener. When I couldn't find it, I went out to the veranda, where I saw the huge container of Dendrite and the many white handkerchiefs that we discovered earlier that night. Bablu had poured out the adhesive on those cloths and inhaled compulsively. 'Perhaps he sniffed it all day,' the police officer had told Ma after we found Bablu. His alcohol breath filled the air, and Ma had moved her face away and murmured, 'I have lived in this city for so many years, never heard of this strange place called Bizi Colony.' Later, standing in the veranda, with the Dendrite container in front of me, I'd thought only thieves could identify the legs of thieves.

Niyor didn't ask me anything else. Not the next day, or in the next few weeks. I wanted to tell him, because he wouldn't pity me, he'd provide me with solutions. As if we hadn't consulted psychiatrists, tantrics, sadhus and women oracles with large red bindis and open hair. Niyor didn't ask me more until he came to spend the night at the filthy Guwahati Medical College Hospital general ward as my attendant after I'd gulped down fifty-nine sleeping tablets.

Bablu had been having extended fights with Papa every morning and every evening around the time I sat down to study. He roamed around during the day. Returned home to fight with us, demanded more money to procure substances we didn't know the names of. By then, he'd stopped going to school. Even when he went—cajoled, threatened and persuaded by Ma—he jumped the wall before lunch break. One day, he broke all the windows of the house. The next day, the chinaware. We stayed under the bed for hours.

That night in the hospital, Niyor didn't ask me about the sleeping tablets, he asked why the hospital authorities had caught me trying to jump from the fourth-floor window two days after they had held me down and pumped out all the molten tablets from my stomach. The tablets had looked like tiny, runny egg yolks, only almost white not yellow. When we were young, we had planned to marry the same girl. Later, we had planned to marry on the same day (two different girls, of course). We had conversations that no one else understood. So I knew that what he was really asking was what this was all about, but that day, I just couldn't tell him. I was sleepy. All I remember is him sitting on the chair beside the bed, staring at me, and the smell of Dettol, and the jute rope that bound my legs tightly to the bed.

By the time my parents had sent me away from Assam to New Delhi for further studies, Bablu had turned into a crackling fire that refused to be doused, demanding to be fed with wood, oil, fat, tears. Each of us took turns to let it feed upon us. Niyor stayed back in our city. He would visit my parents sometimes, help them douse the fire, sprinkle some water with his laughter and jokes, but that was only for a few minutes. How much more could a friend do?

(4)

Ma didn't come to pick me up from the airport when I visited Guwahati during my first winter break. Papa came with our new driver, who spoke a lot while he drove. I asked Papa in English when he'd hired the driver, how sincere he was, if his driving was smooth, if he stole oil. When the driver heard me speak in English, he fell silent. Ma had a thick white bandage around her head, with orange blood seeping through at one spot on the right. When I asked her what had happened, she said she would tell me everything 'gradually', but I wanted to know right away because I knew who was responsible for it. After dinner, I almost cried in my room. Then I didn't because I was ashamed of crying, even though I was alone. But I felt a strange burning sensation in my chest, and a strange, choking lump in my throat.

Ma didn't tell me how Bablu broke the tall, thick juice glass on her head because she'd refused to give him money to buy Dendrite or Eraz-ex. Geeta-baideo told me about it when she came to my room with the bottle of water that I'd need at night and the glass of hot milk that I drank before going to bed. 'If we don't pick up the phone some time, please call Niyor to come and check on us.' She paused and looked around my room. 'At least you'll know for sure if we've been killed by that demon. We are living in the shadow of a constant reign of terror.' Ordinarily, I'd have laughed and asked where she learnt to speak like that, and she would have just smiled, without confessing that she'd picked up the phrases from the laments of my parents who talked like characters from historical plays whenever they were sad.

I woke up the next morning to the sounds of chairs being upturned, slamming wooden doors and Papa's hoarse wailing. The sound of a fifty-year-old man crying loudly is horrible, especially if you were so scared of him when you were young, especially if he was once the apex court whose decisions couldn't be overruled. Bablu was fighting for money again, to buy Eraz-ex, to buy Dendrite, to buy pot.

I went out for a walk across the flyover. Young men from the engineering college were exercising and housewives wrapped in colourful shawls were taking brisk walks with their neighbours, bitching about their in-laws. The morning sun was golden. The leaves that were still on their branches had curled up like centipedes that had been touched. I looked at the streetlights and wondered how I'd managed to study for my twelfth-grade board exams under them, sitting on a step nearby. I had just returned from hospital. Back then, I had badly wanted to blend in with the young crowd that returned from private tuition and coaching classes, who discussed their test papers standing around, cracking peanuts or opening bottles of Kingfisher beer. But I knew I stood apart because I wasn't relaxed like them.

(5)

The summer I returned home after the final year exams, I noticed Ma's eyes had sunken in too deep. She told me insulin injections weren't working for her. 'All because of tension. Have a good look at me, I could die soon,' she declared in a tone that was both grim and funny. Her face was wrapped in sadness, but in a second, she smiled, as if she was laughing at some joke. When Ma acted like that, I didn't know whether to think it was mysterious or amusing or tragic.

But I wasn't worried about her because I knew she had this way of bouncing back. Shahnaz Husain (Perfect Blend of Nature's Secret for Youthful Skin) or Vandana Luthra Curls and Curves clinic (Slimming. Beauty. Fitness.) would take care of her sunken eyes, her darkened skin and the thinning hair. Fact is, she kept herself happy. Under thick make-up and her million-dollar smile, she could hide everything.

I was more worried about Papa. He only slept fitfully. At night, while Bablu slept, smeared in his own urine and shit, after taking twelve pills of different sizes and shapes and colours, Papa walked around our home like an old house fairy. Since he was awake, we couldn't sleep either. Like that time before my school-leaving boards, the summer after my graduation, I stayed up. But he looked so fine. Even if he couldn't sleep because he was scared that Bablu would wake up and break windowpanes, kill Ma, rape Geeta-baideo. He drank warm milk, washed his feet, jogged. In the mornings, when Bablu woke up, they fought. Papa refused to give him money. Bablu called him a dog. Papa said if he was a dog then Bablu was one too. Bablu called him a rapist, a sodomite, which angered Papa. They wrestled. Ma screamed. By then, the neighbours had stopped rushing over. We only called the security when it was needed. After about an hour, when Ma would threaten to jump off the terrace, Bablu would fall at her feet and ask her not to die because she was the 'only person in the world who loves me truly'.

'Then why don't you listen to me? We are trying to help you. Who'd look after you if we died?'

He pleaded, 'Just today, give me the money only for today; I will never consume those harmful things again. Otherwise I am going to kill myself.'

Sometimes, I took out money from my Hidesign wallet, at other times Papa did, or Ma, from her vanity bag or the steel almirah. When Bablu left, Papa looked at his retreating back and said, 'Shanti kinisu!' We are buying peace. Papa often started weeping at this point. I liked it when he pulled out the book of chants for the Mother Goddess and recited.

'Kill him, Mother, kill him! I will sacrifice a black goat if you listen to my prayers. Otherwise, one day I will kill him and go to jail, but then what will happen to my other son, my wife!' Ma told me he'd been praying like that for months and when he heard her telling me, he responded, 'But the Mother hasn't listened to me.'

Geeta-baideo added in her feeble voice, 'If parents wish ill for their children, it really doesn't work. Because they are parents.' Later, she told me she was worried both of them were losing it. 'One day, all of us will run naked on the streets, and you will get to read about it in the Delhi papers.'

I didn't tell her that her 'Delhi papers' rarely published news about Assam.

Instead, I tried to remember that Papa used to be the one who sang songs ('We are in the same boat, brother') as he dusted the books, sticking 'we do not lend books' notes in red ink on the steel and wooden bookshelves.

(6)

The beds stood in a row and the ward smelled of sweat, damp clothes, antiseptic liquid and, underneath it all, something rotten. Government hospitals in India are dirtier than anywhere else in the world, I'm sure, and perhaps this one was the dirtiest of them all. I didn't know what ward it was. When I entered its damp white premises, I had just followed Papa's slouched back. I walked without looking at the large clogged drain on my right, filled with brackish garbage, or the huge festering spittoons where rats ran around, lifting their noses and sniffing the air.

Since it was a case of attempted suicide, no private hospitals would take him in, even though we explained to each one of them, reception after reception, how he'd jumped from the flyover, how he wasn't responding at all, how yellow goo was coming out of his behind and how its stench had filled our Honda City, which usually smelt of rose or jasmine. Papa had been in attendance for the last six days, and Ma wanted him to take a break. 'He will fall sick,' she told me. 'You have to go and spend the night today. Take a book and read. We will get some help by tomorrow from your uncles. Your aunt said she would come to stay.' Not long after Papa had left at around nine, giving me a million instructions on his way out, I wanted to run away, because the five other people in that general ward were staring at me.

'Why are you here? To gloat?' Bablu should have a shave, I thought, looking at the stubble around his seventeen-year-old face. After two minutes, he said, 'Fuck off, I don't want you here: go and fuck Geeta-baideo now that you are done sodomising Niyor's ass. Ja-ja eitiai ja.' I kept quiet. He said again. 'Go and fuck Geeta-baideo now that you are done sodomising Niyor's ass.' I'd noticed he'd developed this manner of 'Go fuck Geeta-baideo, GO FUCK GEETABAIDEO' until it got on your nerves.

'Alright, I am leaving. You are alone for the rest of the night.'

'PLEASE COME BACK!!!'

I was amazed at the energy and the longing and helplessness. I stopped. 'Then stop hurling obscenities. Try to think about other things,' I said.

'I am sorry; you know that's my disease, I like to say such things. What can I do? Give me your hand please.' Tears streamed from reddish eyes.

'Why?'

'I want to hold your hand and apologise.'

'It's fine; I have accepted your apology.'

'No, please let me hold your hand and apologize, otherwise I won't be able to sleep, and I will slash my wrists.'

He spat on my hand when I let him hold it, and when I went to wash my hand, I was in tears. Not out of anger. Not out of exasperation either. I was thinking about Ma, about Papa, about Geeta-baideo. Bablu started to scream for the nurses and doctors when I left the ward. He thought I was abandoning him. The nurses in white skirts and saris tried to calm him, told him to control his anger. When I returned, I saw a tall, plump woman sitting beside him, humming him a song. Saliva dripped from the corners of her lips. She was wearing an ash-grey cotton sari with yellow turmeric stains, but no earrings or even a necklace.

'Come to me, I will sing the song for you too,' she said to me, smiling. A vague smile. 'Everyone must learn this song. It's beautiful.'

The other men in the ward, old and young, urged me to go closer. 'Go near her, she will sing you a song, and we will play the music.'

'Go to her!' the skinny old man with a white beard said, scratching his crotch.

'Go, brother, go,' a young guy in his twenties, who kept looking at the mirror, said.

I had noticed that this man had a mug of water beside his bed; all the other patients had bottles to drink water from but he had a mug too. Occasionally, he would dip his comb in the water and run it through his hair, trying to give it shape. But he never seemed satisfied with the way it looked in the mirror.

At the entrance, I stood transfixed. Soon, they all took out their shiny steel dishes and started to play different rhythms on it, asking me to go to her, listen to the song and learn it. Amidst that cacophony, the woman climbed up on a stool and started to sing loudly, no longer waiting. When I went closer, Bablu muttered to me, as if he were sharing a secret, that I should just ignore her, not say anything, because she was a lunatic. He said, giggling, she'd fight with me if I said something to her.

It wasn't a song. She recited a string of sentences in a sing-song manner about how a woman should give a glass of water to her husband when he returns from work. At the end of the song, she looked into my eyes and said, 'Tell your mother, giving a cold glass of water to your father after he returns from work is the same thing as burning an incense stick in front of Lord Shiva.'

The next morning, when one of my uncles went to attend to Bablu, the rest of us were at home together after days. I told Ma about the incident. She started to laugh loudly, called Papa and asked me to sing the 'song' to him. When I sang, the three of us laughed uncontrollably. I laughed the most—not because the song was silly and funny, but because

I had sung it worse than that woman in the psychiatric ward. Giving a glass of water to your husband / is the same thing as lighting incense / for Lord Shiva / same thing, same thing. Geeta-baideo joined us too, saying she too wanted to listen and learn. Ma said this should become the anthem of our house. When Geeta-baideo laughed, Ma laughed even louder, saying that Geeta's laughter was squeaky like a rat's. Geeta-baideo didn't mind, she continued to laugh squeakily, and I couldn't tell whether she was laughing at herself or the anthem of our house or the way Ma was laughing, holding her stomach, with tears streaming from her eyes. My eyes streamed tears, my stomach ached, I couldn't breathe. I was worried I would pee in the living room right then. For a moment, we couldn't feel the hurt of the doctors' verdict: Bablu would never walk again.

(7)

I decided to walk back home from the high school I taught at, where they didn't pay me too well because I didn't have a masters yet. Walking back would slow down time. It was around 3 p.m. I realised how much I loved the Guwahati winters: not too warm, not too cold, just the weather to spread the folding bed out in the courtyard with a large basket of oranges on it.

Long ago, Ma, Papa, Bablu and I used to do that. We would finish about a dozen in just a few hours. Those were days when we didn't buy greetings cards but made them at home during the winter break with love and care. On the first of January, Ma used to take us to each of our neighbours' houses, where they gave us chocolates or printed cards in return and told us that we had drawn lovely cars and airplanes.

'How was your day?' Bablu asked me with concern when I reached home.

'Good.'

'Why are you so late today?'

'I walked.'

I was yet to get used to his docility. Miracle. That's what the doctor had said, 'A miracle could change things for the better,' because he was 'still so young'. Often, I would tell Papa and Ma that we shouldn't complain, shouldn't talk about suing the doctor because we'd signed those papers, because he'd warned us that there was almost no chance of Bablu's spinal cord becoming normal, because we were eating our meals in peace after fifteen years, because we could sleep peacefully these days.

Papa was quiet. They often worried about what would happen to Bablu when he grew up, who'd wash him, change his bedpan. 'Only parents will do such dirty stuff,' Ma would comment, going on to list names of wives who ran away with other men after their husbands were paralysed because of blood pressure strokes or accidents. I wouldn't ask where she'd carried out that survey. We knew she chatted with patients and their attendants when she was Bablu's attendant at the hospital. All of us would tease her, and say that she should join politics because she would win all the votes with her laughing, chatting and listening to everyone's stories. Maybe if Bablu wasn't the wild parasitic creeper that had been sucking up all their juice, she would have joined politics; perhaps not electoral politics, but she would have become the president of the All India Women Authors Group for which she had been nominated. She had turned it down because of Bablu. I now looked at the new glow on her face. It would put Shahanz Herbals out of business. She hadn't used her creams in weeks. The parasitic creeper was drying away. Was it? Was he?

'Will you teach me how to use the internet?' Bablu moved his wheelchair to the dining table and asked me. I was eating. He told me he tried to Google search the names of good surgeons. But the computer hung. Was there a virus in it? I said casually that he shouldn't visit suspicious sites.

That he shouldn't insert pen drives that just anyone who came home gave him.

'Do you think I will be able to walk again?' he asked.

The doctor had shown us an X-ray of his twisted vertebrae. I still wonder about how he survived a jump from the flyover on to a street full of moving cars, trucks and buses. Sometimes, he cried and howled all night, pulling at his hair until his scalp bled. Or he would scold us all night from his bed. When Papa went to clean him, he'd throw the shit-filled pan at his face. But we could ignore him now. We didn't have to hide under beds and call the cops for emergency help. I'd told Ma to think of it as a radio blaring, and perhaps she did. Papa had started to dust the books once every week again, humming old Bhupen Hazarika songs unmelodiously, reciting Hiren Bhattacharya's poetry: Isn't death an art too? / Carved on the tough rocks of life/ It is nothing less than an exquisite sculpture. Nowadays, when his friends called— friends that Ma was jealous of because she believed male friendships were stronger than that of women—he didn't tell them that 'we are living under a reign of terror'.

'You will be able to walk again,' I told Bablu calmly, putting the plates aside.

'Please tell your colleagues that I just had an accident, okay? Don't tell them I jumped from the flyover, okay?' He kept asking me 'okay? okay?' until I also said, okay.

Even that afternoon, I didn't tell him that I would never tell them or anyone else for that matter—not even Niyor. Not because I was ashamed of Bablu, but because I didn't want to talk about him. There were other things to enjoy, think about: the luxury of wearing just a sweater in winter and walking home, looking at the things that vendors sold on the footpath, calling out to people in their nasal voices, the anthem of that madwoman: Giving a glass of water to your husband … is the same thing, same thing.

म

MINNESOTA NICE

ON HIS FIRST day in America, Himjyoti didn't mind when his new roommate took him to the bathroom, shut the door and showed him how to lock it. 'Push and turn,' he said and then pulled the knob to show it was locked. 'Now push, hold for a sec, turn and then pull,' he said, opening the door. 'Why don't you do it now?'

Himjyoti copied Mike, nervous. He was terrible with doorknobs. A few years ago, when he and his father had gone to consult a doctor back home, Himjyoti had accidentally locked himself in the chamber's bathroom. By the time he heard his father's voice at the door, Himjyoti was highly agitated, having already imagined everyone leaving, his father looking for him on the streets and then filing a complaint at the police station. Finally, the doctor had had to come out, leaving a patient sprawled on the examination table. He spoke loudly across the bathroom door, instructing Himjyoti on the door's locking mechanism, over and over. When Himjyoti eventually walked out, he hugged his father and cried. He was embarrassed about that later. His father had tried to smile, to ease the situation, clearly embarrassed. Yet, he wanted to soothe the nerves of this forever-nervous, oversensitive son.

Himjyoti had always been paranoid. Since he was scared of sleeping under mosquito nets, his parents bought chemical repellents — much to his grandmother's dismay, for she believed they reduced a person's lifespan. In his hometown, they lived in a safe, protected apartment complex. It was old, with moss sprouting from its walls. Once, his mother had latched the main door to go out for a walk, not wanting to wake him from his post-school siesta. He'd panicked on waking up and ended up calling the cops. The police alerted the security agency that guarded their neighbourhood. By the time his mother had returned with vegetable bags in both hands and droplets of sweat sparkling on her forehead, he was faint with fear and foreboding. The cops rang the doorbell soon after she arrived.

People have strange phobias. People laughed at Himjyoti's harmless phobias, and sometimes he joined in too. So he listened to Mike diligently. He didn't want to get locked in the bathroom. He knew that in the US, people didn't drop in unannounced, unlike his neighbourhood in Guwahati, where everyone knew everyone else and dropped in at each other's houses in the evening, staying back for tea and long conversations. His Indian friends who studied in the US had told him about the choking loneliness of this country. About the absence of the kind of friend who would go with you to Cub Foods even when he had work to finish. He couldn't say why people back home accompanied each other to grocery shops, to newspaper stands, to have a cup of tea — why they adjusted so much for each other. The girls even went to the loo in groups. One or two always waited outside.

But he didn't think it was 'cultural', as his American roommate said one day. In fact, he didn't understand what that meant. By then, he had heard so many people using that word to describe something puzzling, confusing or incomprehensible in a foreigner that it had started to annoy him. A few days ago, when the Nepali student in his class spoke out of turn, and a bit too loudly, Himjyoti's classmate

Diana told him that it wasn't rude, it was 'cultural'. But Lakpa had been in the US for eight years and he knew the codes of courtesy. That day in class, he was just very passionate about the topic under discussion. Himjyoti wondered if Diana was afraid to call him rude. Calling the behaviour 'cultural' allowed her to create distance, disengagement and dismissal. It allowed her to not to analyse it, bring it closer.

'No, it's not cultural, Mike,' Himjyoti had corrected him. 'That's how things are in India. We like to be with people, but it's no different if you are a recluse by nature.'

On the first day, Mike had picked him up from the Minneapolis–Saint Paul International Airport. Himjyoti's friend Zutimala, who studied in Boston, told him that settling down in America was like digging a tunnel through the bed of the Atlantic Ocean from the Bay of Bengal with only a pickaxe. She had heard of Indians doing such favours for newly arrived Indians, not Americans. Himjyoti replied that he had heard people in Minnesota were nicer than people on the West and the East Coasts.

'Good for you,' she'd said in an unconvinced tone. 'But make sure you make some Indian friends. They are the ones who will take care of you, come to you when you have fever. Your American friends leave xoxos in your inbox. They are scared of germs. They won't' sit beside you when you have fever and a cold. It's a nation afraid of germs.' She said 'your American friends' in the same tone that little children sang yellow-yellow-dirty-fellow to tease each other.

'Oh, God,' Himjyoti thought, 'why is she always so cynical?'

While Mike was driving Himjyoti from the airport that first day, he said that he had a lot of 'South Asian friends' because his girlfriend was 'South Asian'. When he asked Mike which country she was from, what language she spoke, Mike couldn't tell him. Cheerfully, he said she cooked 'South Asian food on the weekends' and that he loved 'daaal'. The word 'dal' sounded odd in Mike's tongue, somewhat cute. It made the everyday dal so amazing and special that he didn't want to correct the pronunciation.

Himjyoti was pleased to find that Mike's girlfriend was from India. Her father worked in the army, so she had grown up in a major or minor city in almost every part of India: Delhi, Srinagar, Coimbatore, Cherrapunjee, Darjeeling, Ambala, Jalandhar, Thiruvananthapuram, Chandigarh, Kolkata, Pasighat. She spoke Tamil fluently because she went to high school in Chennai. She could make momos because she studied in Darjeeling before enrolling in college and had 'lots of Nepali friends'. She firmly believed that Suniel Shetty was the sexiest man in the world. Her name was Neelakshi Rai. On the first day, when they met, Himjyoti thanked her for making his bed, for writing the wonderful welcome note, in blue and red ink, that was pasted on his door.

*

A week later, Neelakshi didn't laugh at him when he locked himself in the bathroom and screamed, 'Neelakshi, Neelakshi!'

She was making dinner then, but rushed to help. 'Push, keep it in for a while, and now pull,' she kept saying, until he tumbled out of the bathroom in his black briefs, looking terrified. He went back in immediately. But he didn't turn that complicated knob. He just shut the door firmly against the frame.

When he finally came out, dressed, drying his hair with a towel, Himjyoti wasn't annoyed that Mike laughed at him. He knew he'd been foolish. But he didn't like it when Mike asked him, laughing, whether India had such sophisticated bathrooms. 'I have heard you guys bathe in the river?"

'No, we don't! And this isn't a sophisticated bathroom! I don't really know what you mean by sophisticated bathroom because my own bathroom has everything this one has, except the bathtub because none of us like bathing in tubs. I am just not very comfortable with gadgets. I still don't have a smartphone, you know. And I want to buy a new camera such as a DSLR, but I haven't gathered the courage to.'

Himjyoti couldn't understand why he was being so defensive. So apologetic. It annoyed him that he was. He was even more annoyed when Mike asked him, with a polite smile on his face, if people really used smartphones in India, and if computers were popular at all. He looked curious, genuinely interested. Too genuine, too polite, Himjyoti wondered.

Neelakshi ignored Himjyoti's surprised look that probably meant, 'Haven't you told him anything about India?' She was looking away, as if she hadn't heard the conversation at all.

At dinner, they talked about home. Neelakshi said how she missed freshly cooked food, how bored she was of eating frozen items. Himjyoti said that he would soon go to Target and buy all the utensils he needed to cook. Neelakshi said he should buy from Walmart because it was cheaper there.

'I love South Asian food,' Mike said cheerfully, loudly.

Too loudly, too cheerfully.

Himjyoti pointed out that 'South Asian food' is a very vague term. Mike didn't look pleased but asked him what was wrong with that: 'Aren't you South Asian?'

At this, Himjyoti laughed. How would it feel if he called Mike a 'North American' or a 'northern hemispherian'? Mike said in a slightly peevish tone that 'didn't make any sense' and 'you shouldn't mind it because Africans don't mind being called Africans'.

Himjyoti cleaned his plate slowly. He was at the sink when he said that he didn't mind. He was only asking Mike to be more precise. Mike pretended he didn't hear.

Neelakshi said, 'Jeez, you know Anna didn't say hi to me today?' A strange lilt in her speech. Like a drunken man talking to unresponsive passers-by.

'Jeez, how rude! Did she at least smile?' Mike asked.

*

But Himjyoti was able to start cooking only a month later, when he was bored of eating pizzas and frozen food, and after his mother lectured him about the benefits of healthy home-cooked meals. When his grandmother grabbed the phone to repeat the same series of orders, sprinkled with retro Assamese proverbs, he told her that he was running out of minutes.

She didn't understand. 'What do you mean?'

When he explained, she barked out at him, 'WHAT? You don't have time to talk to your grandmother?'

'Aaita, please, we have been speaking for almost an hour.'

She disconnected the phone only when he promised to cook food at home and return to India as the same 'healthy boy we brought up'. Later, his mother called again. She asked him about his friends and roommates; she worried they would 'exploit' him.

'What do you mean, Ma? Will they make me work in the factory and take all my earnings?'

When he cooked that first time, the three of them ate together. Mike said how much he loved South Asian food (too loudly) and Neelakshi had gasped, 'So good, so good.' Himjyoti wondered why Neelakshi didn't tell him frankly that the chicken wasn't very good. The preservative in the Great Value minced garlic had given it a taste and smell that he hated. He ate less than usual. Mike expressed his love for South Asian food one last time (too cheerfully) before dumping his plate in the sink. Neelakshi showed Himjyoti how he could save the food in boxes for heating up and eating later. She suggested that he cook no more than twice a week to save time.

Mike and Neelakshi had gone to his home in Owatonna because it was a long weekend. When they were packing, Himjyoti noticed the spices that Neelakshi was carrying to cook Indian dishes. He teased her that she was visiting to 'do bahurani duty' and impress her would-be in-laws. When both of them laughed, she explained to Mike that 'bahurani' meant daughter-in-law.

With the whole house to himself, Himjyoti played music on his stereo. He sat in the living room, something he couldn't usually do because he felt uncomfortable when Mike and Neelakshi sat there, groping each other, smooching. It made his cheeks warm and ears hot. What would his parents think if they knew about it—though there wasn't a chance such a thing could happen. He had felt that Mike and Neelakshi didn't like it when he sat in the living room or the dining table, a little away from the couch where they'd sit, looking into each other's eyes. Perhaps Neelakshi disliked it more than Mike.

Neelakshi didn't have a graduate assistantship like Mike did since she was an undergrad student. She worked at a shelter home until late at night. And probably slept only three, four hours a day. He wondered how she functioned, how she managed to wake up half an hour before Mike returned from his second job at nine in the evening so that she could take a bath, put on make-up, change into a new dress and wait for him on that couch. Sometimes, she called him up to ask what he would like to eat. She'd keep the cheese melted for him, place the pizza in the oven, so all he had to do was to switch off the oven and pull on the gloves that she'd taken out from the drawer and placed on the desk.

When Mike was very tired, he would drawl, 'Aww, can you please bring it here?'

He made that request often, and she always complied. Neelakshi ate very little. She also used very few dishes because it was she who washed the dishes every day—dishes that Mike piled up on the sink one by one until all the dishes in the house were in use. He made a face when washing the dishes, holding them like fragile crystal dolls. Neelakshi teased him that it wasn't a small bird he was holding, that he had to rub the steel-scrubber hard.

Mike would whine, 'Show me again, daaarrrlinggg.'

She'd show him how, but Mike never said, 'Let me try.' He waited for her to finish all the dishes. She did them, demonstrating how to wash, scrub hard, not do it like he was caressing the cheeks of a little girl.

Sometimes Himjyoti felt sorry for Neelakshi. In the second week after he had moved in, they had a conversation where she'd said her life would be destroyed if Mike didn't marry her because once her visa expired, she'd have to return to the dust and grime of India and work in cities she didn't want to live in. He didn't ask her how her life would be destroyed if some guy refused to marry her. Himjyoti just told her not to worry, Mike would surely marry her, and besides everything had been set up for next year: the cards, the dates, the hall, the wedding gown and the four tubes of Fair and Lovely, the skin lightening cream that she had requested Himjyoti bring along once it was finalised that he would be their roommate. He had contacted them through Craigslist.

When they returned from Owatonna, Mike didn't greet him the way he usually did, the way Himjyoti was now accustomed to. While heating lunch, Mike told Himjyoti that he should open the sliding door that led to the patio when he cooked. He moved his hands a lot when he said that. His voice was a bit strained. And his hands moved a lot. At some point, Himjyoti thought Mike would break into a dance as he spoke. He felt Mike was trying too hard to make the conversation casual, like chatting about the security deposit they made to their landlord. Or about the bathroom knob.

Later, when he was back in his own room, he overheard an argument. Bits of sentences were audible—too audible.

Mike was saying loudly to Neelakshi that he would have to cancel the invitation now. Neelakshi said it was his idea to send around that bleep on Craigslist. Unusually, her tone was sharp, even peevish.

Mike left the house in a huff, frowning hard, but returned quickly. Maybe he'd gone to Walmart because he now had a Lysol Neutra Air Sanitising Spray in his hand, new and unopened.

He didn't acknowledge Himjyoti who had taken his lunch to the dining table. He went around the living room, kitchen and dining room (where Himjyoti was eating) with a frown on his face and sprayed. 'Sorry, this is not toxic. I made sure I didn't spray it near you. Actually, we have guests coming in a few hours, so we need to get rid of the Indian smell.'

Himjyoti said it was all right, but he didn't feel like finishing his meal—the chicken he'd spent two hours cooking so that he could go back home the same healthy boy that his mother and grandmother expected, the dal that Mike loved so much, that he pronounced so wonderfully. It felt as if someone had sneezed on this food.

After clearing his white china plate, he went in to his room and stayed there all day, reading. In the evening, when he came out to make some tea so that he didn't fall asleep and could read more, he saw Glamour magazine open on the dining table. '29 things to do with a naked man' and 'Get your wonder bra today!' In the evening, two of Mike's friends came over.

From his bedroom, Himjyoti heard Mike apologising. 'We have a new roommate, a South Asian, sorry about the smell.'

After a while, he heard a loud female voice, 'Oh, it's cultural.'

Mike said, 'He will learn. We will also learn to adjust.'

Himjyoti wondered what exactly wonder bras were. He thought about the way Mike pronounced dal on the first day when he had driven him in from the airport, telling him about the winter here. He wondered about the twenty-nine things a woman could do with a naked man and smiled to himself.

ব

BEFORE THE BULLET

MINUTES BEFORE THE bullet was fired, Digonto was standing impatiently in front of the officer at the army camp in Teteliguri village, Kamrup district, Assam. He had just returned from a six-year stay in Indiana, United States, having completed his PhD on the effects of neighbouring perturbation on drop coalescence in colloid/polymer mixtures.

The military officer, commanding Digonto to stand straight, asked about the weather in America. About the snow. About 'American women who wear short skirts and fuck men as often as they change bras'. And Digonto answered to satisfy his curiosity: yes, it is cold, it snows, but there are no issues with that because everything is internally heated, and during the winter months, though it is unbearably cold, the best thing is cups of hot coffee. Yes, American women sleep around (he didn't want to debate), change boyfriends like their underpants. The officer asked if he had carried Assam tea with him. Digonto replied, yes, but by the end of the first year, it had run out and he'd had to depend on various blends of American coffee bought from Walmart. The officer said, 'The whites should be posted in Siachen, Kashmir, and they will forget their snow for life.' Digonto said, 'Yes, they should be sent to Siachen, in Kashmir—the highest battlefield in the world.'

The army camp was at the edge of the village. Digonto hadn't known of its existence until that day. It wasn't there when he had left in 1997. Their village had no insurgents, unlike the remote places of Assam. He had been stopped because he wasn't supposed to pass the camp on his bicycle; he was supposed to stop and disembark as a mark of respect to the Sikh regiment officers and soldiers stationed there, and who hung around carrying their AK-47s like khadi-clad leftist students might carry their satchels. Digonto, who did his high school in Guwahati and then left to study in the US, was returning home after six years, didn't know that the once-free village now had certain rules and regulations. Rules that were not made by the village council, but made and monitored by men in olive-green uniform who had set up camp there around five years ago.

When the officer had stopped him, Digonto was puzzled. He'd stopped pedalling and asked, 'Are you asking me to step down?' That was about half an hour before the bullet was fired.

*

About an hour before the bullet few into the air, Digonto de-boarded with his luggage at the Tetelia bus stop. He took the regular route to Teteliguri, where he had grown up, a village he had left less than a decade ago, a village that was named after a 350-year-old tamarind tree. He inhaled the smell he so loved, of dust mixed with dried cow dung. When he saw the newborn calves, he knew he would get to drink 'real milk' after a long time. Milk that you couldn't store for long because it didn't have preservatives. Milk that you needed to boil thrice a day during summers and twice a day during winters so that it didn't curdle, in a village that had no refrigerators.

How many calves had their cow had over these years? But it had been six years: did cows live that long? After six years of drinking Hy-vee and Walmart Whole Milk, he was eager for home milk, unfrozen vegetables and real rotis (not tortillas, which were a poor substitute). But, of course, like every Assamese, he preferred rice.

Digonto was in a hurry to reach home but he didn't quicken his pace, even though he had borrowed a bicycle from a neighbour he met at the bus stop. So he wheeled the cycle and walked. He wanted to smell the forests that the dusty gravel road cut through, and gaze at the light-brown empty paddy fields interrupted only by patches of first-rain grass raising their adamant heads. Soon, it would rain a lot and the fields would be under water, ready to receive the rice seedlings. For some reason, that scene reminded him of his American university. There was farmland around the university too, but no laburnum trees. When he reached the gravel path under the silk cotton tree, a little ahead of the primary school, he mounted the bicycle. He would cycle for a while, walk a little; he would enjoy the fresh air properly.

He shouldn't have sat on the bicycle.

*

Arrangements had been made: he'd sent an email to his friend in Guwahati; his friend's father had called up his uncle's mobile phone; his uncle had cycled two miles (and crossed two rickety bridges: one wooden, one bamboo) to tell his mother, grandfather, brother and sister-in-law the exact date he'd arrive. 'On the 25th, he will land in Delhi, stay back with a friend at the university there before boarding the connecting fight to—'

Konmai, his mother, had interrupted her brother in a shrill, displeased voice. 'What? His friends are more important than his mother who hasn't seen him in six years? I knew this would happen. I knew he would go mad staring at those glass tubes inside that lab or whatever he calls it.' Konmai sat on the blackened wooden chair, on which only men were supposed to sit, and shed tears.

Her mother-in-law raised an eyebrow when she saw Konmai sitting there in front of so many men, but then she thought, let it be, I can understand. 'Get up, my dear.' She caressed Konmai's head with her wrinkled hands, smiling with her wrinkled face. 'Get up, my dear; it's not a big deal. He mustn't have got a ticket in that Flying Ship on the preferred date.'

'I knew this would happen!' Konmai continued to weep. 'What's the point of such university degrees that keep you away from loved ones for so long?'

'But he has sent money. Look, this is not the old thatched house,' her brother consoled her. 'Don't forget the US dollars he sent you over the years, savings from his scholarship.'

Wiping her tears at her brother's consolations, Konmai thought of the small and big sacrifices he must have made to send those dollars that had turned into many rupees when they reached the State Bank in Maloybari village. She never understood the mystery of how a few dollars turned into many rupees. But when was there time to worry about such things? Certainly not after his father had passed away. The debts the man had taken to educate his son, the holes in the roof, raising money for her twenty-year-old daughter's wedding—these were the worries that occupied her, not the mystery of dollars and rupees or small sacrifices.

But his American trip was a sort of lucky charm. The first prospective groom who had come to see Digonto's sister Poree, the young moustached boy who taught physics in the government school a few villages away, had asked them where her brother was, right after Konmai had proudly displayed Poree's embroidery and footloom work.

'Aamerikaa.'

The boy's eyes twinkled. 'What does he do?' he asked eagerly.

'He teaches,' Digonto's mother had lied.

Poree, embarrassed, corrected her mother, 'Actually, he is doing a PhD and he has a teaching assistantship.' But they didn't understand what that meant. Since Poree had passed high school, she could at least repeat the things he wrote to them.

The middle-aged prospective mother-in-law said pejoratively, 'Oh, assistant?' She had a black mole on her upper lip. Four strands of hair sprouted from it; one of them was greyish. 'I guess he cleans desks and benches at the university?'

The boy's aunt, who supported the prospective mother-in-law in everything she uttered, added, 'Must be like our Komol in Delhi. He even bathes his professor's dog, gets them groceries. You have to do a lot of humiliating jobs when you are an assistant.'

Later that afternoon, after they left, Konmai sat in a corner and howled, 'Who will marry you? You just can't keep your loud mouth shut!'

Poree stared at her mother, furious. 'I don't care. Why do you go about bragging that your Great Son is a professor in an American university? He has gone there to be taught, not teach. That assistantship is a part of his scholarship—he said all this very clearly in his letter.'

Konmai didn't like the way Poree spoke. 'I don't know from which angle I am lying. It is not a joke: teaching sums to American kids. How many people from our village have done that? How many from all the villages in this region?' She spoke with such confidence that anyone would think she had travelled around the world, knew just how difficult it was to teach in America. But the truth was that, after she had eloped with Digonto's father at the age of sixteen, she hadn't travelled out of that region. She hadn't even been to Guwahati and that was only about an hour away.

Konmai had predicted that no mother-in-law would like to have a daughter-in-law who interrupted elders' conversations. But so wrong she was. Two years before the bullet went off one afternoon under the laburnum tree, that man with twinkling eyes had coloured the white middle parting of Poree's hair with red vermillion powder. He was proud to have a wife whose brother worked abroad. Proud to have a brother-in-law who sent him an America-bought shirt and a greeting with a hundred-dollar bill pinned inside its pocket.

*

When the soldiers first stopped him, Digonto had told the officer, in Hindi, that he was returning to his village after many years to be with his family. The bicycle didn't belong to him. He had borrowed it from their neighbour at the little kiosk near the bus stop. He didn't tell them that he knew his mother was waiting with cooked food. That his sister would have woven for him traditional gamusas with large flowers on them. That his brother-in-law would have arranged a duck from somewhere, or a turtle, to be eaten with rice. But his movements, his quick, polite and firm replies told the officers that he wanted to be on his way as soon as possible.

When the officer called him a bastard, Digonto looked at him, surprised, and without dismounting, asked him in English why he was behaving like that.

The officer looked astonished, as did the soldier standing beside him. 'Where are you coming from after so many years?' They wanted to see his passport, the official identity card of his university. The soldier told him, 'It's a rule that people dismount from cycles and bullock carts on this path, this path that runs in front of the army camp.'

Digonto dismounted.

'It was also a rule few years ago to take off any footwear, place it on the head to cross this stretch. But the days are peaceful now, so you don't need to do that anymore. The elderly men are not made to frog-jump for kilometres for criminally sheltering insurgents, or serving them meals when they came knocking at the door with guns hanging from their shoulders,' the heavy-built officer said. He then asked Digonto about Assam tea and snow and how cold it got when it snowed in America.

The disbelief and disgust on Digonto's curled lips didn't go down well. They looked at his passport, went through its pages several times. They took a long time, like a cat might smell strange food from several angles before taking a tiny bite.

Digonto wanted the ordeal over with. They had no right to search him like that, he thought. He distracted himself with thought of the dishes his mother would have prepared. He looked at the laburnum tree a little further and felt better. It was fifteen minutes before the bullet, and the crows and sparrows were peaceful, perching, fluttering their wings on the branches. Digonto yearned to stand under the laburnum while the officer interrogated him. The birds had gathered to discuss, as they did daily, which group would occupy how much space among the blooms on those robust branches. So many flowers, so yellow, a tree made of round gold coins. During dark nights, when someone holding a bright lamp walked under it, the tree looked like a tall woman dressed in a glowing dress. He wanted to go closer. They were still looking at his passport.

He asked in English, 'Are you done?'

Giving him a long stare, the officer replied, also in English, 'Yes, you can go now.'

The officer hadn't expected someone in the area to know English, speak in fluent Hindi, to be America-returned. He didn't like the confidence, the stamp on his visa that allowed him to work in the States, the swagger Digonto had when he spoke, when he remounted his cycle. The officers were used to submission, earned from the fear that they had spread in the past five years. Last night, there had been a roundtable conference in the army camp discussing the funds that came for counterinsurgency operations: the money needed to be used up or it would be summoned back to the capital. The best way to use it was by demonstrating corpses.

In this business, only the dead spoke to the government agencies. If there was no unrest (deaths, chases, corpses), the camp would be called off: the camp that laid golden eggs for the soldiers and officers here. Officers didn't like the confidence of men who had been educated in Delhi or London or the US. What if the story of a young local man who didn't dismount from his bicycle, who spoke in English at the army camp in a village where people didn't even know how to speak in Hindi, went around? It could create a hushed confidence in the minds of the villagers.

The officer looked at Digonto's retreating figure. He was just reaching the laburnum tree. The officer's voice was calm. 'Aim at his head.'

'Sir?'

'Do as I say, and if you miss, I will shoot your head.'

The soldier shivered. He didn't want to do it. All he wanted was to go home. It wasn't he who had been complaining about the lack of excitement in the last few months; no chases, no corpses, no gunshots, no skirmishes.

*

The birds scattered. Blood splattered onto the tree trunk. A few petals fell, turning in the wind like a spinning cricket ball. But they would have fallen anyway, because the wind had weakened the hold of their light-green stems in the past few days. The cows were the most frightened, grazing in the fields below, shaking their heads. When they heard the bullet (they didn't see the blood and the creamy brain), they raised their ears and stood stiff, as if struck by lightning. There were a few wobbly-footed calves. Confused, they curled their long tails like touched centipedes, sat down, dropped dung or repeatedly ran in circles round their mothers. From a distance, it was impossible to guess whether they were happy or frightened.

*

Digonto's mother heard the bullet very clearly even though she was in the kitchen, which was filled with the noise of sautéing, boiling, sizzling food. She was, as he had imagined, cooking fish curry for him and the chicken curry that he loved so much.

Poree said, 'Ah, don't worry, why are you shivering like that? The army must be practising.'

Konmai pushed a log of wood into the hearth, took the lid from the iron pan where the chicken curry was simmering and stirred it twice with her shiny, fat steel ladle. 'Hope they are! Nowadays, I have lost trust totally. In just the last ten years, I have seen so many bodies. That ten-year-old boy, what had he done? They shot him because he ran away. What do you expect when you go to talk to a ten-year-old with guns hanging from your shoulders?'

'That Punjabi soldier who is having an affair with Nirmali? He really cares for her parents. He has helped them rebuild their house and even promised to marry her. Next month, his parents are coming over all the way from Delhi to see her. I wonder how they will talk! His parents don't know Assamese and Nirmali's don't know how to speak Hindi or Punjabi. But the boy is nice. The way he respectfully addresses every woman in the village as MaajiMaaji is really heartening.'

Konmai scratched her back with a long twig and pushed it into the fire. 'Yes, this camp's soldiers haven't put their hands on the bodies of women in our village, but in other villages, they have. I guess it's because our MLA is from a nearby village. But don't forget the number of boys they maimed and beat to death four years ago. Don't trust so easily. They speak another language.'

By then, the laburnum flowers had covered Digonto's smashed brain.

দ

THE LOVE LIVES OF PEOPLE
WHO LOOK LIKE KAL PENN

A FRIENDLY WOMAN sits next to Arunabh on the fight. She carries a bottle of green liquid. Must be vitamin water; people here drink a lot of vitamin water, he thinks. She introduces herself as Sandy. Sandy is chatty. She tells him she teaches history in a community college and asks if he is from New York. He says he is from India. He doesn't say that he is from Tinsukia since he is sure she has never heard of his hometown. There is no reason for her to know of it, just as there is no reason for him to visit East Lansing, Michigan, had it not been for this conference. When the fight takes off, Sandy unties her red hair and asks him if he has grown up in New York (for the third time) and he says, no, he hasn't (for the third time). He wants to look out of the window but she has the window seat, and he is worried that if he looks that way, she will ask him more questions, try to pronounce the name of his hometown, fail and laugh, and ask him to teach her how to pronounce it, fail again, apologise, laugh again, and that's how they were likely to spend the next half an hour. So he doesn't look out. He tries to nap instead, but she wakes him up when she has to use the restroom and apologises profusely. It is okay, he says, though he is irritated. It is not her fault, he thinks. When she returns, she requests the air hostess for a bottle of chilled water and some peanuts, then calls her again and specifies that she wants roasted but unsalted peanuts. The air hostess says she will check and get back to her.

It would have snowed in Michigan by the time they reach, Sandy says. She is worried about the snowfall, but he says it is okay, he has never seen snow and would love to see and feel it for the first time. She is surprised and asks him how far the Himalayas are from his hometown, and he says, very far, as far as Alaska. He doesn't mean it and he doesn't care if she believes it. They talk about climate change and online dating, about travelling to Greece when they have money, about the lack of tenure-track jobs. But he doesn't tell her that he is new in America, that small-town Minnesota, all this conversation about the impending winter, people saying jeez and sorry and thank you all the time are his first glimpses of the country. He doesn't tell her that he is going for a conference, that when he signed up for it earlier that year, he didn't know the venue was in the middle of nowhere, or that his flight would be so small, with only two rows of seats, small enough that a strong gust of wind might cause it to crash.

There are no shuttles from the airport to the university. The cab costs 185 dollars. He is upset but has no choice. It is November and the air is nippy, even chilly. At the airport lounge, Sandy and Arunabh wait together for their rides after she calls her boyfriend. When her ride arrives, they shake hands and say their goodbyes. She smiles and says she will find him on Facebook, to which he nods and smiles back—the kind of smile that doesn't show teeth but conveys measured warmth. Then he adds that it would be good to connect, and worries if she will get his last name right: Borkakoti. She says she loves India and has plans to visit once she is married. She is going to marry the man who is coming to pick her up.

'And I am not marrying the person who is coming to pick me up,' he jokes. Before leaving, she pauses and asks if she could tell him something.

'Yes, sure.'

'Alright, you know I have been thinking since I met you and I wasn't sure if I should say it.'

'Oh come on, just say it.' He laughs.

'Alright, alright. You know, you remind me so much of Kal Penn. He is like my favourite actor! I mean, he has grown older and put on a little weight, but he is absolutely adorable. And I think you look like him, quite a lot, do you know?'

Arunabh's heart sinks a little. 'Hah!' He forces out a smile and says, 'Never thought about that.'

Sandy's lips form an inverted U. It is the kind of expression that people make when they know they have said something offensive but also know that it isn't very offensive and this show absolves them of it. But Arunabh is silent for several seconds, not knowing what her expression is all about. She rolls her eyes, moves the inverted U slightly to her left, and adds quickly, as if to fill the awkward silence, 'As in, a younger, handsome, Kal Penn Moody?'

He wants to say, actually, it is Modi, not Moody, but all he can say is, 'Oh, haha.' He knows his smile isn't reaching his eyes. So he exerts a mild force on his lips to keep up the smile for a little longer and adds another 'haha'. But he can feel his smile and the goodbye expression slipping. He tries to bring them back and wonders if he is looking like a fool. He decides to reject her friend request on Facebook even if she gets his last name right.

'See you. Will connect later.'

'See you,' he says. He doesn't want to look like Kal Penn.

He isn't flattered that she thinks he looks like Kal Penn. His cab driver Jim can't pronounce his last name either. 'Mr Bukkake? Hi, I am from Clinton County Cabs.' Arunabh tries not to laugh and wonders if Jim knows the meaning of bukkake. He doesn't mind because there isn't a chance that they will send each other friend requests. Also, he doesn't mind because there is nothing to mind. Jim wears a blue denim jacket, has black hair and one of his front teeth is missing. He has tobacco stains on his gums but smiles broadly and is extra friendly. His name is easy to pronounce. He is six feet tall.

It is five in the evening. The pre-winter November air in Michigan is sharp on his face and neck. Jim mumbles that it is going to snow and starts the car. Inside the car, Arunabh takes off his cap, sits comfortably, pulls down the zip of his woollen coat, looks at the sky and hopes it will snow. He wants to see snow, touch snow and walk on snow. He doesn't say that to Jim, of course. Because then Jim would know that he is new in America. Jim turns on the heating and Arunabh feels warm and sleepy, but he doesn't want to sleep, even though the journey is going to be long and lonely. In twenty minutes, they have left the city behind, and for miles and miles, he sees no human beings or houses.

Not even birds. He looks out, enjoying the fall colours since there is nothing else to look at. The warm, comfortable car makes him feel lazy, and he doesn't feel like revising his conference paper or making calls or checking Facebook.

Years later, when he speaks about this journey, he won't remember whether the cab drove through downtown East Lansing, cutting through the campus of the large state university, or even if East Lansing had a downtown at all. He won't remember whether he saw Jimmy Joes, Papa Johns, Olive Gardens, Apple Bees, Burger King and other restaurants. But he will remember how the trees were running away from him. He will remember that he didn't want to look like Kal Penn, and that he studied his refection in the rear-view mirror, and more than once had considered asking Jim whether he saw any resemblance to Kal Penn. And he will always remember the fall colours, his first fall in

America: the gold, the yellow, the orange, the red; the blue sky that was slowly turning grey; and his yearning for snow.

Soon, it will be dark and he will still be wondering if he actually looked like Kal Penn. He is sure he doesn't want to look like him.

*

At the reception desk, Arunabh meets a young man who is also attending the conference. He is training to be a journalist with a programme in New York City. He grew up in New Jersey but was born in Delhi, where Arunabh had moved to study for a few years. They don't hit it off because the young man says he is working on a project that tries to understand, not justify, the philosophical reasons—he uses the word 'underpinnings'—behind the attack on artists by the Indian right-wing. Arunabh cannot imagine how that qualifies as a subject of research. Why, he wonders, does this man stress that his research is not trying to justify the violence on artists and writers. He takes out his credit card, swipes, signs the receipt, thanks the receptionist, and asks him how his work does not condone something heinous. The young man develops a cranky tone, an unpleasant swagger. This man who 1) is training to be a journalist 2) working on a project that tries to psychoanalyse and philosophically understand why the conservatives attack artists and shoot writers and 3) was claiming the project wasn't trying to justify violence, is called Adit.

'I thought this conference was about Human Rights and Literature,' Arunabh quips. He decides not to attend Adit's session.

Adit asks him if he would like to grab a cup of coffee. Arunabh has no idea why he agrees, but they walk to the other end of the room, where some people who look like Serious Conference Attendees are sitting. On a desk, there are four large coffee dispensers: hazelnut, dark roast, medium roast, decaffeinated. There are cookies and pretzels and green apples and bananas on a large tray engraved with the name of the hotel. Adit asks about Arunabh's paper and he says, oh you won't be interested. He hears the sarcasm in his own tone and decides he must dial it down. It is cold outside but there is no sign of snow.

Arunabh tries to change the topic. 'I don't understand the point of decaffeinated coffee. Isn't it just brown water?' They agree on something finally. Adit chuckles. Arunabh doesn't understand why this man has taken a liking to him.

'America is a funny county,' Adit says in a deliberate Indian accent.

'Now, come on, tell me about your paper.'

'Why don't you come to listen to me tomorrow?' He is a bit irritated now.

'My god, you are adamant.'

'One has to hold one's ground, don't you think?'

'I will come for your paper. I like to listen to people who make a career out of dissing their country!' He winks, raising a thumb at Arunabh.

Perhaps he is trying to make the threat sound like a joke, or the joke sound like a threat, but Arunabh finds it neither funny nor threatening. He doesn't smile back, doesn't wink back, just leaves the lobby. He looks outside and hopes it will snow at night. He will then open the window, take a picture with his new smartphone and share it with his friends in India. So beautiful, he can already hear them exclaiming. His friends in Assam have never seen snow. His mother is worried Arunabh won't be able to cope with the snow and catch a cold.

*

On the third floor, he looks for his room. Most American hotels feel like mazes to him, so easy it is to lose one's way.

He remembers the conference hotel in Madison, where he could never find his room on the first try, and this hotel feels the same. When he finally locates his room, he cannot unlock it. He tries, with his laptop and duffel bag hanging from his right shoulder. Then he gently places them on the carpeted floor, and tries again. He tries for a very long time, and he is tired and unhappy, and realises he hates people like Adit and doesn't want to look like Kal Penn.

'There is a trick to opening that door.' A husky, resonant voice.

He turns around. Never in his life has he seen such a beautiful woman. An indigo scarf covers her head. Everything else she is wearing is pitch black, except the bright, silk muffler around her neck, giving her a radiance that matches her expressive eyes. He almost drops the keys. She says, 'May I?' but doesn't wait for him to say yes. She takes the key from his hand and unlocks the door in a second.

'Oh my god, that looked easy.'

'But it is not.' Her voice is deep and sonorous. She speaks from her heart, he thinks, and immediately considers the thought stupid. He smiles.

'I am sorry—? Did I say anything funny? I am sorry if I did. I didn't mean to—'

This time he smiles broadly. 'No, you didn't say anything funny. I was just thinking of something else.'

'Oh, I am sorry. I thought—' He does the rude thing. He interrupts. 'Any chance you are from Minnesota?'

For a second, she looks stunned. Then she bursts out laughing. It is a loud, throaty, crackling laughter, a confident and happy laughter. He laughs too.

'I am not gonna ask how you know.'

'You don't have to,' he says. 'Hi, I am Arunabh. I live in Shakopee.'

'What a small world!' she says, pushing her own door open.

He notices how skilfully she unlocks her door. She knows the trick well. He wants to tell her not to go. To stand there and chat. She pushes her door open and waits. 'I am really sorry, I haven't even told you my name.' She comes forward to shake hands with him and the door shuts behind her with a thud. 'I am Adayomi.' She gasps as soon as they shake hands. 'Fuck. My door is shut, and the key is stuck in the main switch of the room!'

'Oh no, I am sorry. Don't you have a spare key?'

'Yes, I do.' She feels the pockets in her jacket. 'I am so sorry I swore.' Her fingers rush through the pockets but return empty. 'But I think I left it on the table inside. I went to get some coffee downstairs and left the second key on the table. Oh no, I am so sorry.'

He pushes his door open. For a second, he isn't sure whether he should invite her into his room so she can wait while the hotel staff arrive with their master key. If he invites her in, he may come across as creepy. If he shuts the door in her face, it would be rude; rude to the person who helped him unlock his door, rude to the person who says so many sorries, rude to the person who is also from Minnesota. And she is beautiful. He wants to hang out with her. He wants to be her friend. In a second, he has decided. He props the door open with his luggage, and says he will be back after calling the main desk. She waits at the door. Perhaps she can see him from there, picking up the phone on the bedside table and speaking. Maybe she can also see the white curtains and beyond that, through huge glass windows, the yellow streetlights, the racing cars, the orange coloured tree that was shedding the last of its leaves to welcome the winter.

'I am so, so sorry, you must be so tired,' she says.

'It is alright and you don't have to apologise. It happens to everyone, I am sure.

She rolls her eyes. His door is still open, and if she wanted, she could look outside, she could look at the orange leaves falling and the group of people who were walking on the road. She says, 'I hope it never happens to me again. I am sorry I am delaying you. The dinner is at eight-thirty and it is almost seven-thirty. You won't have any time to rest.' She folds her arms and looks at him.

'That's alright! I am Arunabh, by the way. I am from India. We don't say "sorry" and "thank you" that much, so it is a bit odd for me.'

She smiles and looks down at the brown carpet. It has chrome-yellow patterns.

He adds, 'You know, I have to say this, my god, Minnesotans apologise all the time. My friend Kate apologises for apologising too much.'

She shakes her head and laughs again. This time it is not throaty. It is a soundless laughter, her body shaking with it. A bit of her red muffler comes undone, revealing her neck. It is longer than he expected. 'I get that a lot. I came to attend school in Minnesota eight years ago and have been living there since. But my family is still in New York. And guess what, I now think them rude!'

Now Arunabh rolls his eyes. 'I am not sure if it is really about being polite. My awful roommate leaves these stickers on my door, which I find after a long day.' He puts on a poor American accent to mimic his roommate, 'I would really appreciate it if you could please spray the anti-bacterial liquid on the kitchen counter after you make tea and then mop it with the kitchen rolls.'

'Seriously?' Adayomi is as if offended on his behalf.

When a housekeeper comes with a set of keys, Arunabh hates him for arriving too soon. He wishes the man had brought the wrong keys. He hopes there is something wrong with the key and that it takes longer to open the door. But he opens it just fine, says 'Don't worry, it happens to the best of us' with a too-wide smile, and leaves.

'Have a comfortable stay,' he drawls.

Arunabh wants to kick his ass. 'I didn't even ask what your paper's about.'

'Oh, don't worry, it is not scintillating.'

How skilfully she unlocks the door and pushes it open. She has long fingers and her nails are painted blue. 'Shall we meet at 8.25 downstairs? It will be good to meet the rest of the presenters.'

'I think so.' She doesn't leave. 'It is very cold outside. So bundle up.' She sounds like a caring friend—like his new friends in Minnesota who regularly offer rides for winter shopping. 'It may even snow.'

'Ah, well, it is two degrees already.'

She gasps. 'What!'

'Oh, wait, I mean in Celsius. I am still getting used to Fahrenheit. It doesn't make sense to me. Why do you guys have to do everything differently?'

'Don't blame me. My father is Nigerian. I was born in Canberra and we moved here when I was fourteen. I am all for Celsius, only I don't understand how that works!' Then she stands there for a few seconds more. As if she is waiting for him to say something. She looks beautiful when she smiles.

'I see,' he says. 'Don't tell me your paper is on Chinua Achebe.'

She laughs again. Throaty and loud. The laughter of a joyful person. He wants to see snow, touch snow and walk on snow.

*

There are sixteen conference delegates at the hotel. They meet in the lobby but soon break up into groups of four or five. Some of them had arrived earlier in the day and already formed their own circles. Arunabh's group walks to the pizza restaurant nearby. He doesn't like pizza but goes along anyway. It looks like a cheap place, and he doesn't want to spend a lot of money. He is still converting US dollars to rupees in his mind, he is embarrassed to admit. There is a woman called Elena with them who moved to Boston several years ago from Wyoming. She makes sure everyone knows that. And that she is working with a famous academic, and that she ran into Derek Walcott several times while waiting for the elevator. Adayomi and Arunabh sit next to each other. She turns to look at him and a smile forms on his lips. He sees that her lips have formed a soft inverted-U. He looks away, worried he will burst out laughing, and the woman from Boston who met Derek Walcott won't like that. Elena is full of energy, loud and excited, like a child high on sugar. If she could, she would run around. If she could, she would do sit-ups. Mow a garden. She dominates the dinner conversation, and like many people here, uses a few words repeatedly.

They are: excited (variations of it), amazing, cool, awesome and that sucks. She is the one who reads out the menu, asks everyone about their preference and then places the order. She says that if the waiter walks around the table asking people what they would like to eat, it would drive her nuts. She repeatedly touches her blonde hair and rattles off the list of things she is allergic to and what she likes or dislikes eating and also provides a list of pizzas she thinks are amazing. She strongly recommends the pizzas she likes. When Tara, from Mumbai, wants to order one with olives and tomatoes, she asks if Tara is sure that she wouldn't want to add pepperoni. Tara says no. She asks again, 'Are you sure?' Later, when they wait for the food, she talks about her ex-boyfriend, the athletic sex they had, and the perils of online dating in America. Arunabh doesn't want to know any of this.

Adayomi is quiet. Arunabh is quiet. Adit is not so quiet. Tara is wearing a sari. She is smiling so much that he wonders if she is jet-lagged because, between Elena's anecdotes, she manages to say that she landed in Chicago only that afternoon. After Elena finishes talking about her sex life and dating life, she wants to know about everyone's papers and responds with one of her stock words. Arunabh feels he is in the middle of a panel discussion and she is the moderator—a bad one. She uses the word 'awesome' in response to Arunabh's abstract. Tara is the last one and she speaks for at least four minutes and fifty seconds. He wonders if everyone has now decided not to go to her panel the day after. She continues to speak until Adit interrupts her with a question that was clearly meant to disrupt her, not out of any curiosity. Elena takes the window to respond to Tara's narration of her abstract and paper and the research trips she made. She uses a different word: 'Interesting.' Tara looks disappointed. Perhaps she wanted to hear one of those superlatives that Elena had been using.

'So, you did you grow up in Nigeria? Kedu?' Elena asks Adayomi. 'I have read a lot of Nigerian novels.'

'No, I grew up in Paris and New York, and I don't know the meaning of kedu.'

Elena's disappointment is visible. She stops mid-sentence, her lips parted just wide enough for a fly to enter. She pauses like that for a few seconds. 'So how did you get interested in Nigerian literature?'

Adayomi fumbles. 'Oh, I mean, everyone has heard of the civil war and we have all read Achebe.'

Arunabh says, 'So your paper is actually about Achebe.'

'Yeah,' she says in a bored tone. 'All Nigerian English PhDs are about Achebe, you know.'

Tara bursts out laughing. She is so loud and her voice so thin that it startles the baby on the next table. The baby starts to cry loudly, looking at Tara, and the mother is annoyed.

She tries to whisper, 'I am sorry. I am just jetlagged.' She fails at whispering. It seems she is a generally loud person.

Elena is unrelenting. She asks Adayomi, 'But, I mean, your upbringing must have helped you gain some interest in Nigerian writing, right?'

'My father is an engineer. He doesn't even read the papers, forget Achebe. And my mother is a nurse. She had no time to read books and she is Bangladeshi.'

Arunabh looks at her, pleasantly surprised, and she responds with a soft nod that no one else can see. Perhaps, it is a nod to the bond that they had suddenly found in their common South Asian-ness.

'Oh,' Elena sounds defeated. But she bounces back to ask cheerfully, 'You must have visited Nigeria, though?'

'Once.' Adayomi sips her Coke.

The pizzas are on the table. The waiter asks if he can get them anything else. Arunabh knows that he will come back and ask if they are enjoying everything and everyone will say 'food is great', 'awesome'. How are people always so cheerful and enthusiastic here? He doesn't want to be cheerful and enthusiastic all the time. He wants to see snow. And he is still irked by Elena's questions.

'Elena, but you must have grown up in Somalia, right?' Arunabh asks her.

She looks shocked. 'Of course not.' She places her piece of pizza on the white plastic plate. 'Oh no, not at all. Why do you think so?'

'No, since you are presenting your research on Nuruddin Farah. How did you get interested in him?'

Elena's annoyed expression is enough, so he wants to leave it there; he has made his point. He allows her to concentrate on her pizza and contemplate what just happened. But Tara ruins it. She places her water bottle with a thud on the table, covers her mouth and coughs a little and says loudly, 'You're killing it,' and bursts out laughing. Water dribbles from the corner of her lips. She uses a tissue to cover her face but a stream of water falls on her chest. She swallows the remaining water in her mouth and laughs loudly, gasping. The baby starts to cry again and the mother mumbles something and gives their table dirty looks. Tara continues to laugh, 'That's a good point, Arunabh; that's a good point.' The baby cries louder. Elena eats her dinner in silence and avoids him for the next three days.

*

Twenty minutes later, they are walking towards the university campus, laughing. Adayomi laughs in loud gasps, interspersed with 'oh my god' and 'you are too much'. She asks, 'Why did you do that?' But he is laughing too and is in no state to respond. The large red-brick buildings of the university welcome them. It is 9 p.m. and they should go to sleep if they are to wake up in time for the conference, but they walk on. She says she owes him a treat. He says he will accept on one condition—they'd have to sit on one of those large plastic benches outside and eat. She says it is cold and adds, mimicking him, 'Two degrees Celsius.' But later, when she buys him baklava, they sit outside. They eat slowly.

'What did you think about that guy? The other Indian guy,' she asks him.

'Oh, he is an ABCD.'

'I know that term—it is not a nice term, I know. My mother uses it a lot!'

She laughs again. 'I didn't bring water, don't make me laugh. When I laugh a lot, I choke.'

'Okay, then I won't tell you what ABCND means.' She gives him a look full of question marks. 'American Born Confused Nationalist Desi.'

'What?'

She gasps, laughs. 'Where do you even learn these things?'

'Tell me about your mother. How did your parents meet? And which part of Bangladesh is she from?'

His voice is full of excitement, tone quite loud. 'She's from Chittagong. It is a long story, but my father tells everyone that he met my mother in bed.'

'What does that mean!' Arunabh laughs so much that he has to put down his plate of baklava on the bench. 'Sounds like a poor joke!'

'Yes.' Her eyes become large. 'My sisters and I had banned that joke in the house, but later we found out that my mother really loves this awful joke, so the ban was lifted. Now we are filled with dread when someone asks him where they met. He had an operation in a Dubai hospital where she was working as a nurse. That's how they met.'

Arunabh nibbles on the sweet, shaking his head, uttering a muffed 'gawd, parents'. He takes a sip of his coffee. 'I think Adit is going to come to troll me during my presentation!'

She is drinking decaffeinated coffee. He doesn't tease her. The temperature is dropping fast. He tightens the muffler around his neck. She sits in a heat-preserving position: arms folded, hands inside the warm coat pockets.

'I don't know what am I doing here with you. We should go! My blood is going to freeze,' she says.

'You are buying me baklava in appreciation of my brilliant trolling of Madam Elena.'

It starts to snow and Arunabh stands up. He feels the snow on his hands and watches it melt immediately. The snow looks like cotton swabs, and he watches the flakes melt as soon as they kiss the ground. He hears a mild sound: kit-kit-kit. It is the sound of snow falling on warm ground and melting on contact. But snow is relentless and adamant. It falls again. Kit-kit-kit. Kit-kit-kit. He is amazed at the sight and sound of it. Adayomi stands next to him.

'Let's go', she says, and he says, 'Wait, let's wait.' She is loud now. 'You will see so much snow in your life in Minnesota that you will want to return to India. You will hate snow. You will have to memorise the size and design of your friends' coats in order to recognise people during winter. Fuck, it is cold.

'Adayomi.'

'Yes? I am leaving if you aren't coming with me!'

He wants to say, I know you won't go, but asks, 'What is the meaning of your name?'

'You want to know that now?'

'Because I am sure there is a meaning.'

'Will you fucking go if I tell you the meaning of my name?'

'Yes, I will.'

'I think it means something like She Brings Me Joy or something. I don't know. I don't speak Igbo. Although I do know the meaning of kedu, but I just didn't want to talk to that stupid woman.'

They start to walk back. She is still in the heat-preserving posture. 'And what does your name mean?'

He doesn't want to tell her that his name means sunrays—sunrays that bring mornings, that melt snow. He doesn't want the snow to melt. Arunabh, whose name means sunrays, looks straight into her eyes and says, 'Promise me you will meet me in Minneapolis. I will tell you the meaning of my name.'

She smiles. Her eyes dance. She holds his hand as they walk into the lobby. When he takes her in his arms, he believes his kidneys are moving around his body and his heart has stopped forever. At that moment, he realises, he could die, and there would be no regrets.

ফ

FOR THE GREATER COMMON GOOD

NEERUMONI WAS THE first one in the family to suspect the bark manuscripts. Anil had stared at her in silence. Where on earth had she heard of books being haunted? She said firmly that it wasn't the soul of her dead husband, his father Horokanto, who was troubling them but the souls trapped in the manuscripts. She stood up and went out to the one-acre pond behind her house, bamboo creel in hand. She would spend some time there. Washing the rice, vegetables, clothes and vessels from the afternoon's meal wouldn't take long. Chores done, she liked to change into a petticoat, tied just above her breasts, and swim for at least an hour.

Winters aren't harsh in Teteliguri, not like the villages at the foot of the Jaintia Hills on the Meghalaya border. The wind from the hills enters every nook and cranny there. Meghalaya is the abode of clouds. The white clouds descend as quiet as cats' paws, and soon people are in the middle of a fog, even before the cat's tongue can scrape their bones. No, here, in Teteliguri village, things are better. There are huge paddy fields. There are many houses, many people in these houses. Here, the climate remains warm and comfortable. Of course, when the trees in the stunted hills that guard the village start to sway, there is a storm. But the chill reigns only on nights when the winds freeze the stones, and then carry the bite of it into the houses of the village, an uninvited guest. That's why, when Neerumoni first said she was hearing things, Anil had suggested it was the wind. It was usual for the wind to knock at the door, hover over the straw roof of their thatched hut. They had never finished reinforcing the walls with mud. Back then, she was confident that it was the soul of her spiteful husband, Horokanto, who had many unfulfilled desires when he died in that accident. He wanted to return to the mortal world, she thought. In the process, he would rob them of all peace.

Eventually, Anil took her seriously, as did most other women in the village. They prayed. They left a meal with Horokanto's favourite dishes on the western side of the house. But the manuscripts still opened and shut in the middle of the night (mainly on Saturdays and Tuesdays) all by themselves. Nor did strange souls stop troubling Neerumoni: they left earthworm mounds on the food she cooked, and strange handprints on the bedsheets she washed with khar. And one day, when she had cooked duck meat with banana flower, they dropped a ball of curly hair in the pot.

Gradually, those murmurs, faint songs, the rustle of bark as the manuscripts turned their own pages, invaded the dreams of Neerumoni, and Anil too. On lonely afternoons, when everything was quiet, those sounds were louder, quicker, restless. One night, Neerumoni woke up, disturbed by the choric melody of the singing crickets. She saw four lanky men standing over the small wooden box where the manuscripts were kept. They were trying to open the lock with a knife that had a blue plastic handle. When she shouted at them, they turned towards her, grew black wings and few off through the ceiling, leaving it undisturbed. Her screams woke up the rest of the family, and she told them one of the figures had worn a long green dress, the other three white turbans and dhotis. They looked as if they were from a royal family. They didn't wear ornaments though.

No one believed her. Her suspicions were fortified when she saw one of the manuscripts take the shape of an old man in her dreams. He was crying, asking her to set him free, telling her that he was trapped there by mistake, unlike the other souls who had committed sins. He promised never to disturb her if she freed him from the fetters of the spells in the bark manuscripts. When she said that she hadn't trapped him, she wasn't holding him there, he got angry and screamed, called her a liar. Anil laughed it away. But Anju, who would have said many sarcastic things about her mother's superstitions, who would have fought with her even a month ago, was quiet.

Anil looked at Anju and felt again that, after she was raped, he required inhuman strength just to look at her face, let alone her eyes. She was sitting in a corner when her brother and mother were speaking about the old man trapped in the manuscripts, fingering the crisscross of welts on her wrists, the result of being tied to a bed with steel threads ordinarily used to tie bamboo. Everyone was away. It was the death anniversary of the village headman's mother. Neerumoni had asked her to come along, tried to tempt her by saying that she'd get to eat porridge at the function, but Anju said that Biren would come to leave his baby son with her. His wife was away and the little one wouldn't sleep until Anju sang him a lullaby. Even that day, Neerumoni reminded Anju that she shouldn't forget that Biren was after all a man. Though he was her first cousin, the sudden intimacy between them over the last two years was the talk among certain sections of the village.

But Anju was a popular girl. Everyone loved her. Almost every household in the village was indebted to her in some way or the other. 'Anju, would you please weave this mekhela for me? I won't pay you the full price, but I will give you something as a token of love.' Anju turned into Mother Teresa when phrases such as 'token of love' were mentioned. 'Anju, could you come to our house tomorrow morning? I have asked everyone in the village, but you know how the girls in our village have become after the cinema hall opened in Sonapur, they are afraid their hands will melt away like a leper's if they so much as touch the mix of cow dung and loamy soil. Who else will I ask?' Anju nodded vigorously, agreeing with the old woman. 'Anju, don't you dare forget to come a week before the wedding. You know there is no one else I can trust with keys to the money, the ornaments, with supervising … oh, you are such an angel, what would I do without you?!'

So while some tongues were wagging, others remained quiet. Why should anyone suspect the relationship between first cousins? Those tongue-waggers said 'first cousins' in a dismissive, mocking tone, and suggested that Biren was 'woman-hungry'.

Thus, the day after Neerumoni found an unconscious Anju lying on the bed with bleeding wrists, the whole village blamed Biren and accompanied a near-crazy Anil to the police station to lodge a complaint. Biren was in jail now for raping Anju. And inside that haunted house, where books with souls created strange noises, a new Anju lived with a constantly growing belly. This new Anju didn't speak, and often cried silently.

Slopp-slopp-slopp! The sound brought him back to the present. His mother had rushed in and was now standing in front of him, her adult son, in wet clothes that had become translucent. She hadn't brought her bamboo creel back and looked terrified. When he asked what was wrong, she told him that a rough, hairy hand had pulled her down by the leg while she was bathing in the pond. 'I didn't see it, Anil, but it was a man's hand. Hairy. It's the manuscripts, I am telling you.'

*

Anil's father Horokanto learnt sorcery from Neerumoni's father Doityo-burha long before the Indian army camp in this village became an integral part of the lives of people here.

As the result of a small disagreement with his own father, Horokanto left home for good. He took shelter in the house of his closest friend, Neerumoni's brother Nilambor. The next day, when they were having breakfast in the kitchen, her father had asked him what he was interested in. Horokanto replied that he would like to learn the art of sorcery from Doityo-burha. It wasn't an easy art, said the man who was known across seven villages as a great magician, the man who controlled the souls of many rowdy ghosts, forced snakes to come crawling back to suck poison out from the wound of a dying man. Doityo-burha sipped his hot milk and looked at the younger man. But Horokanto was determined to learn. He promised to follow all the rules and regulations. The old man with the long white beard warned him again: if he neglected the rituals for even one day, the bark manuscripts that held the trapped spirits of wild but dead men would strike him dead.

In fact, when he was finally a master of the art, Horokanto managed to imprison a bidaa, a ghost who would be under his command like a genie in a bottle. But the only way to keep the bidaa under control was to give him more and more work. In the next room, Neerumoni, who was a seventeen-year-old girl then, laughed and told her elder sister that it wasn't difficult at all—one could just send the bidaa to a desert and ask him to dig as many wells as possible.

Neerumoni saw Horokanto for the first time three days later. He was swimming in the pond wearing a white gamusa around his waist. It clung to his buttocks. She remembered a long-forgotten feeling. The strange and disturbing pleasure she had felt when her pot-bellied thirty-year-old cousin, who had come to invite them to the rice ceremony for his second son, had pushed up her petticoat, taken out his penis, rubbed it against her inner thighs, asked her to hold it and move her hand slowly up and down. When he started to moan strangely, she got suddenly scared and fled, but not before he had kissed her lips, pushed his tongue inside her mouth and sucked her upper lip. That was her first time with a man. After a long time, seeing Horokanto, she wanted to lie down beside him.

They had sex for the first time on a rainy winter afternoon, just after the grains were harvested. It wasn't the sort of sudden winter rain that farmers worry will blacken the leaves of the potato. The day had been windy since morning. Clouds gathered little by little in the sky, leisurely, like people trickling into a wedding reception. Her grandmother had advised everyone not to spread out the new grains for drying in the courtyard that day because it might rain. Though it was winter, the sun was strong—you had to drink at least two glasses of water after a half-hour walk. When it finally rained, everyone was ready for it, and had taken to their beds, or settled down near the hearth with a drink of tea. The cold, the fresh smell of water on earth, the wind: it was ideal. When she reached her house, the quietness of it and the empty veranda seemed to instruct her to go straight to the room that Horokanto shared with Nilambor. Inside, he was lying on his stomach. She latched the door. He looked at her, startled, and tried to smile, but she knew he found her sudden entry odd. She started taking off her clothes. When she was finished, she moved to Horokanto who was staring at her with rapid breaths. Later, lying naked beside her, he had pulled her closer and said he had never seen a more beautiful woman in his life. They smelled like coconut water.

After four months of random, wild lovemaking, behind the house at midnight, beside the pond early in the morning, in the mud of the Tamulidobha river, behind cowsheds, on hay stored to serve as fodder, they eloped. They knew her father would rather kill her than let her marry him. He stole most of the manuscripts. Her father died ten years later; by then, Nilambor had died unmarried and Neerumoni had given birth to three daughters and a son. Anju was her first-born. Anil her second. On his deathbed, her father had met Horokanto finally, had given him the rest of the manuscripts, cautioned him to use them carefully and for the good of humanity. Doityo-burha also mentioned that since he had eloped with Neerumoni against her father's wishes, he would not be able to use the spells when he most needed them. 'It's not my curse. I have seen that Fate has decided this punishment for you. These manuscripts are powerful but they are unforgiving if you disrespect them.' Horokanto died in an accident about thirty years later. That morning, he had fought with Neerumoni and hadn't worshipped the ancient books for the first time in his life.

*

After the army crackdown, everybody in the family began believing Neerumoni's claims about the bark manuscripts. The previous day, rebels had blown up a bridge that connected the village with the National Highway and Guwahati. In the explosion, three Indian soldiers from the battalion stationed in the village were killed. The tall, longhaired Punjabi soldier, who always wore a red turban and was respectful towards women (unlike the others), lost his hand. The intensity of the explosion caused it to fly and land on the roof of the village fisherman's house. His wife was sitting in the courtyard having her lunch at the time. A stream of blood fell on her shoulders (some say most of it fell on her rice and face). At first, she thought a bird had shat on her clothes, but the shit was red and the bird looked like a hand. For a while, she stood staring at her roof where the hand was, and then fainted. When her neighbours found her an hour later, sprinkled water on her eyes and brought her back to her senses, she vomited and started to wail hysterically. Everyone in the village went to see the wailing woman and the clenched fist, with five golden rings on its fingers—stones meant to ward off the evil influence of powerful planets. They sucked in sharp breaths through clenched teeth and wished Horokanto was still alive. When

Dilipram came, they fell quiet. He was the only sorcerer left in the village now to take care of spirits and snakebites and barrenness in married women. They were convinced that the soul of the Punjabi man was refusing to leave.

The army crackdown happened the next day. Scores of soldiers came in jeeps and surrounded the village. Their boots were loud as they ran towards the hamlets. Someone had started to play the drum in the village prayer hall, and it boomed like the announcement of a war. Neerumoni's neighbour, Bibha, came running to tell her to flee. 'Save yourself and your family members, forget the belongings.' Neerumoni stood frozen for a moment, not knowing how Anju would run with that bulging stomach. Then the two of them hurried along as fast as Anju could manage, hoping it was just a false alarm, hoping that, in the village's central meeting ground, everyone would say, go back, nothing is wrong.

But Neerumoni saw that all the young men were running towards the forests. She saw women, children, girls and old men running across the fields to get to the next village. They would cross the Tamulidobha river, dry in winter. She too ran that way with a heavily pregnant Anju, thinking how Horokanto and she had made love on the banks of this river, in the mud, like two buffaloes, one morning. It was the monsoon, and the river that ran beside the passionately love making couple flowed with force, creating whirlpools, voluptuous with desire and laughter. Neerumoni heard gunshots. She turned back. Someone said it was Hiren and someone else said, no, no, no one has been shot. They started to run again.

They returned the next morning, after spending a worried night in Maloybari village across the river. Each and every house had ransacked. There were boot prints on clothes, white bedsheets were soiled brown and black. Food was strewn around. Beds upturned. Tables broken. Chairs piled up in front of the courtyard and burnt, both plastic and wooden. Mattresses left out in the rain or set on fire and still smoking. Mud walls broken down. Earthen pots lay shattered in courtyards. As they were putting their houses back together somehow, the village folk could hear the cries of Prodhan Mahatu, the village milkman. He had forgotten to untie his twenty cows, and the army had shot and killed all of them. Their corpses were lying in the cowshed, stinking of blood and the greenish dung that had come out along with their intestines.

In the haunted house, Neerumoni asked Anil, 'Every single object in this house has been thrown around, but look, the bark manuscripts are where we had left them. They have even thrown away the mustard oil lamp that we lit in front of the manuscripts, so why didn't they try to open this locked wooden chest?' All of them believed that the chest would have been broken and the manuscripts removed, but those were haunted manuscripts, they didn't need legs to return to their original place. They imagined that the soldier who disrespected the manuscripts was dying slowly of some strange disease. For the first time, Neerumoni and her family felt safe because of the presence of the bark manuscripts. All these weeks after Horokanto's death, they were petrified, unable to solve the mystery of the sounds. That night, Prodhan Mahatu went to the army camp, stabbed one soldier and set one of the camps on fire. They shot him dead.

*

Dilipram wasn't a great sorcerer. Now middle-aged, he had once learnt most of his charms from Horokanto even though he was apprenticed to an old sorcerer in Hatimura village, Mayong, for about five years. He lived in the old man's house and worked on his fields in lieu of fees. The sorcerer had given Dilipram the teeth of a male crocodile, the dried hands of a pregnant female monkey, severed legs of mating lizards, snakeskin and many other indispensable things required in the art of serious sorcery for the greater common good. When Horokanto was alive, Dilipram would occasionally come to him with questions: 'Do we use a pregnant bitch's morning urine to make this potion?' 'I made the potion for cobra bite with khar, but I'm worried about whether the concentration is strong enough.'

The people in the village had thought Dilipram would inherit the bark manuscripts. In fact, Neerumoni had offered him the books but he refused. She must know, he said, that those manuscripts had a soul and they always chose their owner, just as her father was once chosen. So was Horokanto—or why would he fight with his father and come to stay in their house to learn sorcery when he had belonged to such a rich family? It's all decided 'above', he had told her with conviction, pointing to the sky. 'You will get signs.' One day she would have to let go of the manuscripts so that they reached the rightful owner. That person could even be Anil, or one of her future sons-in-law.

Now, when Anil told him about the strange sounds that shook their house and robbed them of their sleep, Dilipram suggested that they take out the manuscripts every Tuesday and Saturday, spread them under the sun (if there was no sun, the veranda would suffice) and light a mustard-oil lamp, offer some white or red flowers, and pray to the Gods of the ancient books, requesting them not to trouble the family. 'Try it,' he said calmly. When Anil stood up to leave, Dilipram told him that, if it didn't work, he should return on the night of the twenty-second Saturday with a new steel plate. They would go to the cremation ground. Anil started to walk away. The breeze lifted the light cotton cloth that covered Dilipram's flabby body. He turned and told Anil that he had this strange feeling that one of the trapped souls had become very powerful since they hadn't been controlled by spells for nearly a year now, since Horokanto's death; that soul might be trying to take corporeal form to fulfil its worldly wishes.

In the deathly silence that followed, Anil felt he could hear ants moving across the courtyard. He broke out in a cold sweat. Dilipram added that the soul could be trying to take birth through Anju, so they would have to kill the child as soon as it was born if the first remedy didn't work. Anil decided that he wouldn't tell his mother about this last part. She would worry unnecessarily.

On the way home, Anil passed Prodhan's house. A strong stench of rotten animals rose from it. He rushed to get ahead of the smell and vomited. Tearing off some leaves from a eucalyptus tree nearby, he inhaled the scent of it until he felt better. The village would have to do something as soon as possible, he thought, wiping his face with the cotton handkerchief that Anju had woven on the waist loom before she was raped. After Prodhan was shot dead, his wife and two daughters vanished mysteriously. They must have fled to a relative's home. They didn't even wait to receive the body. But that was wise—the army would have killed them too had they gone to ask for his body. It was the villagers who received Prodhan's decomposing body. Before that, young men and women from the city had come with pens and tiny notebooks and cameras that made loud sounds. The army flew them in a helicopter, and took them on a tour of select localities. They would then report that no villagers were harmed during the operation. Some of them came by car, and the army helped them cross the river on boats.

Anil stopped by the grocery shop to buy some red lentils that his mother had asked for. The shopkeeper wrapped it in an old newspaper. Anil didn't notice the bloody picture that was printed on it.

On reaching home, he apologised to his mother. They should have believed her. He conveyed what Dilipram had told him, except the part about Anju's unborn baby. Neerumoni said, 'Let's wait and see what happens.' They would worship the manuscripts for twenty-one Saturdays and Tuesdays.

She went in to ask Anju if she needed something. But the girl just wept soundlessly, which she did a lot these days. Neerumoni knew why. After she was raped, for a long time, Neerumoni had blamed her for the incident: Didn't I tell you not to roam around with Biren too much? Wasn't I cautioning you for a long time until it finally happened? You destroyed your life, and ours too.

After talking to Anil, Neerumoni shivered. She didn't know if she would raise Anju's child or kill it with the help of other women. Two more months left! It was already February. What would happen if she gave birth to twins? No, no, as if one child isn't enough trouble … Would she be able to stuff a handful of salt into the infant's mouth and take his life? Wouldn't this child be her first grandchild?

When she went to the kitchen and unwrapped the lentils, Neerumoni saw the bloodied face of the slain man printed on the newspaper. She trembled, and imagined the blood being mixed with the lentils. Should she wash the lentils again to remove that blood? She felt queasy looking at the blood, the rose-pink lentils. Then she realised it was Prodhan's face: distorted with anger, full of the pain of losing twenty cows that he had reared like his own children: cows that came running to him whenever they saw him, red and brown and white cows that liked to rub their heads on his back; cows that licked their calves' balls and ears; cows that he rebuked if they chewed the clothes hung on the line to dry; cows that had the most beautiful eyes in the world.

She called out to Anil to ask if it was really Prodhan in the photograph. He looked at it and said, yes, that's him. He read the headline out to her.

TOP MILITANT GUNNED DOWN IN TETELIGURI VILLAGE

She threw away the lentils. They didn't have lunch that day.

The day Anju spoke a full sentence, that too in her normal tone, Neerumoni couldn't believe her ears. In the nine months since the assault, she'd only heard her daughter cry in agony and impotent rage. Anju was whispering something. At first Neerumoni thought it was the sigh of the rain-bearing wind from the hills. It had been raining hard for a few weeks, an early monsoon. The previous morning, Neerumoni had noticed that the edges of the veranda had disintegrated. Probably the first wave of foods would arrive soon too.

Neerumoni went to Anju's room and asked what she was saying. Anju said she had seen a child with eyes that shone like fames in her dreams last night. When her mother heard this, she was sure the manuscripts were now troubling her daughter. She looked worried and promised that she would send Anil to Dilipram's house again as soon as he returned. Neerumoni sat beside her daughter. Anju extended her hands and pressed her mother's, wept and said she didn't want the child. As soon as it was born, she would shove a handful of salt into his mouth.

It was dark outside. As if the sky had covered itself with a black shawl to keep away the chill. Even though it was still early in the day, a soft blanket of darkness settled on the wet roofs, over the rain-drenched trees, paths, stones and red soil. Neerumoni held her daughter's hands. Through the window, she looked at their dog who was shivering in the sudden chill, curled up on hay in a corner of the cowshed. She noticed that the small wooden suitcase shook mildly — was it throbbing? Moving? — as if someone were trying to escape. She could feel her breaths become heavy, shallow.

Anil didn't return until late afternoon. After serving him lunch, Neerumoni mentioned Anju's dream, and Anil was too stunned to speak for a while. Then, slowly, he told her what Dilipram had cautioned him about — that one of the souls might have become too powerful and could be trying to attain physical shape by possessing Anju's child. Neerumoni thought about Anju's dream and whispered: he must have already taken possession of the unborn.

By the time Anil left for Dilipram's house, it was raining harder. He passed the Tamulidobha, suddenly becoming aware of its noisy waters. The hilly tributaries had given her a new life, youthful blood. It was as if she were mocking the village, or perhaps trying to wake people from their stupor, warning them of something. He also crossed Prodhan Mahatu's house. Last month, the villagers had cleaned up the mess. They didn't know what to do with his land and property, and left everything the way they found it. Even the clothes. One of the men had entered the house and told the villagers that, on the hearth, there was still a container of cooked rice and huge steel pots of milk that had curdled, grown fungi, turned green and yellow and brown, and were letting out another smell that was difficult to describe. Now, Anil noticed, wild creepers had completely covered the house, the huge cowshed and even the bamboo gate. There was not a glimpse to be had of the mud walls or the wood in the windows.

When he returned home, it was evening. When he told his mother that Dilipram had advised him to relinquish the manuscripts, she asked him if he was hiding something from her again. He lit a fire, and as he warmed his hands at it, Anil told her that he wasn't. In fact, he should have told her everything the last time too. A storm had broken out, running through the village like a madwoman. Their thatched hut started to vibrate.

Neerumoni wondered aloud if they would be able to go out. Anju's abdomen was hurting. Anil said that that was even more reason to go, because Dilipram had told them they had to act immediately, even if lighting strikes down the whole village and the hills. They would have to do it on their own, before Anju gave birth, otherwise the soul would be born in their own house, and no one could predict what it might do.

As they were leaving the house, Anju's water broke. She screamed, but in the wild roar of the dusk thunderstorm, they didn't hear her cries. Anju crawled down from her bed, breathless, and lay down on the green mattress on the ground, spread her legs and waited, wondering if she would be able to do it all alone. At first, she lost consciousness.

Anil looked at the betel nut trees moving like drunken men weaving their way down a village street. He wondered if one of them would fall, killing them both. He held the wooden suitcase firmly with one hand and the umbrella over his mother's head. But they didn't have the umbrella for long. The wind was strong, like the spring storm Bordoisila. People believed the storm was the soul of a newly married woman rushing back to her mother's house with her long hair open, destroying everything in her way: huts, trees, cowsheds and crops. The storm that evening was as mighty as the impatient Bordoisila. So when they finally heard the wicked laughter of the youthful river, they were relieved.

The riverbank was slippery, and below, the water flowed furiously. Anil saw a wooden chair being carried away. Will they go really? The souls? It had to be done by Anil's hand, since he was the heir to his father who died without choosing the rightful owner of the bark manuscripts, who couldn't train someone, who did not give away the knowledge of those books before dying. After they had emptied the box into the tempestuous waters, Neerumoni told him that someone breathed on her cheeks and she heard a sigh. Anil didn't say anything but she stressed that it was warm, as warm as it could be in that chilly evening. Then he said, it was just the wind, just the sound of the wind moving across the leaves and over the waters. On their way back, they didn't worry about Anju, but only thought about Horokanto — the husband, the lover, the father. Before opening the gate to their compound, Neerumoni said, 'You know, even my father found most of these manuscripts in a wooden box. Things just get repeated.'

'What will happen now?'

'They will travel, maybe even to the sea, in search of another owner.' Inside the house, Anju was lying unconscious, a newborn between her legs, slick with blood. Neerumoni took a sharp knife and cut the cord. There was absolute silence. She waited; she patted on the boy's back. It didn't cry.

Anil wanted to say that it'd be too soon, too good to be true, but he kept quiet. He looked at his sister's face, called to her. He wanted to show her the baby before he buried him.

The soil at the back of their house would be soft like mud now. Digging a deep hole would be easy. Neerumoni sniffed. The air smelled of fresh mud. She wondered why the baby's face reminded her of her dead father who was hurt because she had eloped with Horokanto.

ढ

THE UMRICANS

A MONTH BEFORE you move to America, your aunt is admitted to a small hospital in the northeast Indian town you live in. She needs an eye operation. That year, your mother had bought a new Hyundai i10 car and hired a driver. He prefers to go by 'pilot' — 'driver' is diminishing but 'pilot' has gravitas, he thinks. He drives both of you to the hospital. Your father is away in Delhi on an official tour. He phones regularly

In the hospital, where the nurses are extra courteous and ward boys are extra helpful, your brother-in-law expresses disbelief at the news that you are moving to America with a scholarship. He is the kind of person who attended a three-week refresher course at Delhi University and tells everyone that he has degrees from there. He is like the driver who thinks he is a pilot. 'We have not haard of this place Minnesota,' he says with a shrug, as if Minnesota is a bad smell, as if speaking in English makes him sound more authoritative about American geography. 'We have haard of New Yok and Los Angles and Sicagoo, but not this place called Minnesota. Are you acsually going to Amerika?' You want to correct his pronunciations, but you don't. Your mother isn't pleased. She starts to say something, but you gently press her hand and she remains silent. On the way home, she says you should have let her speak. You laugh. 'Oh, Ma, leave it.' Then both of you laugh at your 'Delhi Educated' brother-in-law.

A month later, your parents see you off at Guwahati International Airport. It is a small airport, and international only because an occasional fight departs for Bhutan. You have travelled to Delhi so many times in the past year for the American visa interview that the guards recognise you. They don't examine your ticket. They wave at you and request that you do not forget them when you reach 'Aameyrika'. You watch your parents' faces and know that they are trying hard not to cry. Later, on the flight out of Delhi, on the flight that is taking you to the US, you wonder if they knew that you too were trying hard not to cry. You go to the lavatory and bawl. When the air hostess serves wine, you ask for whisky.

*

At the International Students' Orientation, the staff teaches you how to say 'sorry' and 'thank you'. They say, when someone says they are sick, you should say, 'I am sorry.' The students you sit next to are north Indians. They are the kind of loud and patriotic north Indians you normally wouldn't be caught dead with. You are ashamed that you are laughing with them. 'What other funny things these Umricans are going to teach us?' the handsome Punjabi guy with a beard asks you before switching to Hindi, and you like the way he pronounces 'Americans'. Hindi is not your language. But you don't mind that he assumes you speak and understand it because you are from India. You laugh with the Punjabi guy. A few days later, you are surprised that you are drawn too to the Bangladeshi students—the Bangladeshis whom you grew up slightly hating for migrating in thousands to your already over-populated state. You talk about rice and fish curry and Durga Puja and Bhupen Hazarika's songs and feel guilty. You hang out with Shahed—the student from Dhaka—who challenges you to eat a burger without making a mess on your plate. He borrows his friend's car and drives you to Minneapolis where both of you eat at a restaurant called 'The Taste of India' run by Punjabi-speaking Pakistanis. Garlic naan and butter chicken, gulab jamuns for dessert. You both almost weep with joy. When you offer him money for gas, he scolds you, 'Don't be so money-minded like the Umricans.'

A month later, Shubham (the Punjabi guy) and Shahed (the Bangladeshi guy) are your closest friends. When you fall sick in October, they turn up at your apartment instead of sending texts such as 'xoxo', 'get well soon' and 'I am so sorry you are sick'. They make you spicy soup, sleep on your couches and make lists of girls they want to fuck. A week later, you don't tell your mother about those lists, your bad health, about the winter that is coming too soon. Instead, you tell her that there are two seasons in Minnesota: Winter and Preparing to Fight through Winter. She laughs. You think about how she was silent at the eye hospital when you pressed her hand. You are suddenly surprised that she understood your touch. You wonder if she cried as soon as you turned to x-ray your duffel bag at the airport. You hide in the bathroom and cry. You don't tell Shahed. You don't tell Shubham. But they look at your reddish eyes, slap your back and buy you a beer. They don't leave you alone because you are sad. They force their presence on you, and you like that and you joke that the Umricans would never do something like that because they are very respectful of your personal space.

*

Mike, your roommate, has an Indian girlfriend called Neelakshi. She often spends the night in your flat, mostly during weekends. He tells you that this year has been amazing for him since he has never shared an apartment with a non-white person before. And how he is thrilled to have more International Experience with an Indian Girlfriend whom he started dating three months before you arrived. With your permission, Mike changes the apartment's Wi-Fi user name to 'Diverse Club'. You are amused and annoyed. He asks you questions that you don't like. He asks whether your hair grows straight up like the African-Americans and whether you straighten your hair. He is astonished that you can speak English 'so well'.

Since he is an English major at the university, he corrects your 'fortnightly' to 'every two weeks' and your 'out of station' to 'out of town' and is completely horrified when you use the word 'preponed'. You say, it is Indian English. He asks, 'Does that even exist?' He tells you about the new Pakistani student in his class who doesn't wear a skullcap and expects you to be surprised. He is surprised that you are not.

Mike changes the Wi-Fi username to 'South Asian Station' because he thinks it is more apt. You pretend to find it funny, but you think that he can be insufferable. In December, when his grandmother visits, she asks if you are a Muslim. She is happy to know that you aren't. She gives you a piece of lemon cake and confides in you that she worries Muslims are going to take over America soon. You nod. You don't get annoyed. But you are annoyed when everyone wishes you Merry Christmas on the last working day before Christmas. You rant about it to Shubham and Shahed. It doesn't bother them.

*

Neelakshi moves into the apartment. The good thing is that the three of you now split the rent and power bills. The bad thing is that the frequency of their noisy sex increases to at least four times a week. You are woken up by their moans and gasps, the sounds of their bodies slapping, the creaking bed, and a lot of 'yes-yess-yess' and 'you-like-that-right?'. You are not sure how to broach the matter. You decide you hate American houses. You complain that there is no privacy. Shubham and Shahed find the situation hilarious and ask if the lovemaking gives you a hard on. One morning, you find Mike sleeping on the couch on top of Neelakshi, without his boxers. Later, Shubham says you should have drawn a smiley face on his bum with a black permanent marker When you call your mother, you don't tell her that you are annoyed with your roommate. You tell her that Mike is good and takes care of you. You make her talk to Shubham and Shahed. She speaks to them in broken Hindi and fluent Bengali. You proudly say that a lot of people from Assam know Bengali—something you would never admit to in India, even though it is a fact. In April, your mother falls sick. She has hypertension and your father rushes her to the hospital. She is moved to the Intensive Care Unit. Her blood pressure is unstable for twelve hours. The doctors pierce a gelatin pill and place it under her tongue every three hours. You spend a lot of time on the phone with your father. You feel guilty that he has to manage alone. You are their only son. You look at flights online though you know you can't afford them. Your father asks you not to come because he knows you can't afford the cost of a flight; after the medical bills, he cannot either. The pilot helps your father. His wife cooks meals for your parents. He stays in the hospital day and night so that your father can use the car when he needs it. You are the first person your mother wants to talk to when she is out of the ICU. 'I won't die without seeing you,' she chuckles. Your grandmother tells you not to worry, to eat well and return to India as the same 'healthy boy we brought up'.

You smile. You wonder if her eyes are welling up like yours are. You remain sad for a long time. You share your anxieties with Neelakshi and Mike and Shahed and Shubham. Mike asks if the driver will charge your parents overtime, and you want to slap him hard.

You snap, 'It is called goodwill. Everything is not about money like here in America.'

'But you are exploiting the driver, you should pay him overtime!' Mike says hotly.

Neelakshi does a bit of contextualising. 'Why must every act of kindness be returned with money? You can return it instead with kindness.'

Mike is not pleased. He says he doesn't get South Asian Culture. Neelakshi says something funny. She has acquired a risible American accent. She throws her Rs and rolls her tongue a lot. The rumour among the Indian community in the university is that Neelakshi is seducing Mike because she wants an American passport.

Back in India, your mother is brought home. People say such horrible things, she complains to you on the phone. 'Your brother-in-law says that he knows an old couple who live near the airport. They have four children and all of them have moved to Aameyrika. When the man died, there was no one to cremate him.'

You sense your anger rising quickly. 'Well, Ma, If Delhi Educated people don't know what to say when a person is sick, who will?'

'Don't become Aameyrikan like other Indians, please come home when you can. We will arrange the money. Okay?'

You laugh, but you know that your mother is expressing her deepest fears.

In May, Mike sends you an email in bullet points. When a Minnesotan sends an email in bullet points, you should know that they are very mad at you, your friend Amy tells you, and laughs so much that she almost chokes on her bottle of sparkling water. You decide not to write back but talk. At the apartment, Mike looks through you. When you say, 'We need to talk,' you feel as if you are his boyfriend, broaching a break-up. He turns around and says in a calm voice that he would prefer to be emailed. You say that you would prefer to talk because you have no time to respond to his slanderous allegations by email; you have papers to write. Neelakshi assumes the role of the mediator to save the situation from becoming worse. You debate with her in Hindi and English. Your voice rises many times as Mike hovers. You tell Neelakshi that it is not possible for you to spray antibacterial chemicals every time you use the kitchen, and that you will get your own dishes because Mike uses most of the dishes and expects Neelakshi and you to wash them.

In June, you move to a different three-bedroom apartment on Warren Street, sharing it with Shubham and Shahed. You have a nice portico that overlooks a lake. Loons swim in the lake. Their yodels wake you up from your rare siestas and regular power naps, but you don't mind, because you like the sight of the large, cheerful duck-like birds. The three of you have gained a lot of weight because your dinners are usually cheesy pizzas at the on-campus cafe where you wait tables. Bad cheese. Bad bread. They are not bad to eat, though. The three of you join the gym and run for hours on the treadmills because you worry that no girl will sleep with you. But you don't date. You don't even hook up. You want to get good grades. You want to get a good job and that's why you are working towards a degree in Information Technology. You want to bring your parents to America and buy them meals at Olive Garden and your favourite, Chipotle Grill. Soon, you learn how to drive. Every Friday, you borrow a car from a friend and drive to Minneapolis. You have also learnt the bus routes. You don't get lost in the city. Sometimes you go to Dinkytown alone and sip coffee, enjoying the weather and the youthful vibe. You are surprised that you yearn for the sun. Amy says that you have now become a Minnesotan.

During your sophomore year, you visit the website of the Indian-American community in Minneapolis. You attend one of their gatherings. They screen a movie called Pardes where the actor Amrish Puri sings the line 'I love my India' and you can't stop weeping. You notice that others are weeping too and stop feeling like a fool. You want to buy a dinner coupon. It is thirty dollars, much higher than you expected, but you still pay. While having dessert, you meet a family from your state, Assam, who introduce you to other families from Assam, and the other families from Assam invite you home. You find a Little Assam in Shakopee, where several Assamese families have settled. They are from small and big towns. At their parties, women cook food and hang out separately. They are all in their early forties and the women are all light-skinned and slim. The men are overweight and friendly. You suspect they are all monogamous and boring. You drink whisky with them and they tell you about relatives they have lost in bomb blasts and skirmishes. They hope the militancy in beautiful Assam will end one day. They share their first experiences in America and you are startled at how similar the stories of these people in their early forties are to yours. When they get a little drunk, they sing Bollywood songs. They are terrible. Even you sing better, and you are quite bad. Yet, you like hanging out with them, even though in India you wouldn't be caught dead with people who sang so badly.

*

In your fourth year in America, Neelakshi and Mike get engaged. They invite you to their engagement party. Your old apartment on James Avenue is now their home. You ask Neelakshi what you can bring. She teases that you have turned into an Umrican and scolds you for asking what you can bring. At the party, Neelakshi, Shubham and Shahed have to explain repeatedly to Mike's American friends why, in South Asia, it is almost offensive to bring food when someone invites you to their home for a meal. Mike says the Wi-Fi username of the house is still South Asian Station, and Shahed gives you a look that makes you want to hide under the table. Shubham is worried that if Mike's American friends fall sick after eating the spicy chicken curry, they will sue Neelakshi. He says she should send an email listing all the ingredients used so that they know what they are consuming beforehand. Mike laughs and asks him not to worry. He is so happy.

You meet Roshan at Neelakshi's party. He is her friend from Nepal. Roshan is a college dropout and has been living illegally for a few years now. He works at the local Korean restaurant for three dollars less an hour than his co-workers. After the party, he gives you a ride back to your apartment on Warren Street. Shubham and Shahed don't join you; they go downtown for more drinks. Roshan wants to discuss how Neelakshi has seduced Mike for an American passport. You avoid the discussion. You are put off by the disdain on his face. And surprised because you know that he too wants an American passport, because he too wants to become an American. 'Neelakshi sucked his dick for the passport.' You want to scream TMI, like the Americans do.

You thank him when he halts the car near Atwood Apartments, where you live. 'Why don't you suck an American dick as well? Don't you want an American passport too?' You slam the door.

Every day, you call your mother. You have saved some money, you tell her. And you could come down that winter. But she asks you to come in summer after your graduation because that will be a longer visit and more worthwhile. You want very much to go home, but you see the wisdom in your mother's advice. She will now tell everyone in the neighbourhood that you wanted to come but she forbade you. It is a chance to show off that you wanted to come and that you have saved money by working. She won't tell them that you wait tables. She will tell them that you assist one of your professors.

*

Six months before your graduation, your mother has a mild heart attack. Your father and the pilot rush her to the hospital. Later, your father tells you that, on the way, she kept pleading with him not to inform you. That upsets you. You want to ask her about it but can't, because you aren't supposed to know. You start keeping the phone in your pocket all the time. At night, you put it on loud mode and leave it next to the pillow because you are worried your father won't be able to reach you. You don't sleep well. You wake up at night to check messages on WhatsApp, to check if there are missed calls. When you cook or you read in the library, you check the phone screen frequently. You start to hear false rings and feel false vibrations. You know you are imagining things but don't tell anyone. Nor do you talk to anyone. You don't visit the free counselling service on campus because only Americans go to therapists, not Indians. Because you have friends who come home to take care of you without worrying about germs. And yet, one day, you visit the therapist. You wear a hoodie and cover your face with a scarf because you are so ashamed. 'How does it make you feel?' the therapist asks, looking calmly at you through her thick-rimmed glasses. You are amazed that you think of them as 'glasses' now, not 'spectacles'. You say that to the therapist.

That night, your father tells you that the pilot's family has been very helpful, like a son and a daughter-in-law. They clean and cook for your parents. You feel they are doing things you should have done. You weep at night. When it is dawn in India, you pick up the phone and call your mother and ask her why she didn't tell you that she had a heart attack. She laughs and says that she won't die without seeing you, because you will have to touch her temple with a flame to set her soul free of the mortal world. You shout at her for speaking rubbish but she just laughs. It is March and you browse MakeMyTrip.com. You use up all your savings to book a round trip for a date in May. You tell her that you are coming home soon. That you found a good deal. How much, she asks. You tell her the amount in rupees.

After the conversation, you walk out to the drawing room. Shahed offers you a cup of tea. You tell him that your worst fear is that you won't be home if something happens. He doesn't ask what you mean by 'if something happens'. He understands. He understands because he is not American. He understands because that is also his worst fear.

When your worst fear comes true just a week before your trip to India, it takes a very long time to sink in. You receive the news during your finals week—two weeks before your graduation. You have exams to write. You have worked hard for this for the last four years. You have waited tables late into the night and then stayed awake until dawn drinking cups of coffee and completing class assignments. When you received a B minus, you went to the Writing Centre several times to rework your drafts because you wanted good grades, you wanted to make the best of everything. Your parents are cutting corners to educate you in America so that they might one day come and see snow, see the Statue of Liberty, eat burritos with a lot of sour cream and guacamole.

When you hear the news, you walk out of the library, where you were writing a take-home exam. You clutch your bag hard against your body as if someone will snatch it from you. You are surprised that you are not able to cry and that you are worrying more about graduation, about how you don't have enough money in your Wells Fargo account to book a ticket immediately. You regret that you bought the expensive gown and hat and the tassel so that you could send your mother photos from the Graduation Day ceremony. Someone calls you from home. You will never remember who it was. Maybe a relative who has taken charge of things. The person talks about preserving the body in a morgue. She will feel cold, you whisper. You feel like you're choking. Like you can't breathe. It is early May. It is still cold in Minnesota. You sit at the cafeteria where people are busy and noisy. You call your father and ask him, what is the meaning of these rituals? What is the point of freezing the body for several days just so you can touch her temple with a flame at the cremation ground? She will feel so cold in the morgue. She hated being cold. Your father weeps. You wonder how he must feel because you are not able to feel anything. You walk out into the cold and sit on a blue plastic chair, shivering. He is still on the phone with you. You tell him you will not come, because there is no point now, and when he hangs up, tears stream down your cheeks, and you mourn the young boy inside who has died along with your mother. You mourn because you have become someone you have always despised. Shubham and Shahed try to take you to the apartment. But you say, like they do here in America, I am fine, can I please have a moment? They notice your steely resolve and say, I am so sorry, I am so sorry, and leave you alone.

হ

HIS FATHER'S DISEASE

THE FIRST TIME Anil brought a man to his room, his mother
Neerumoni went to the backyard and sat on the stone beside
the red hibiscus for a long time. Then she picked up the
brass pot and went to the large one-acre pond to take a long
bath—swimming from one end to the other, splashing in
the water. She didn't want to hear the lovemaking sounds.

Forgetting to change out of her wet clothes, Neerumoni
sat on the banks of the pond and wept. 'He has acquired his
father's disease,' she thought, mourning her only son. When
she figured it was time for those 'disturbing sounds' to have
ceased, she walked back slowly. To her horror, mild moans
were still audible from his room. She left the fresh pot of
water on the clammy kitchen floor, went to her bedroom,
lay down on the bed and wept.

Those sounds were all too familiar. When she was
seventeen years old, Anil's father had come to learn sorcery
from her father, a high-caste brahmin. Quite surprisingly,
her father, known as the stingiest person in the village,
appointed Horo as the new caretaker of his farms and agreed
to teach him sorcery for free. Later, she had come to know
that Horo was close to her younger brother, Nilambor, who

had put in a special request to that effect. Much later, after she had settled down with Horo and had one child on her back and another growing in her womb, she came back from the fields one afternoon to hear sounds of two men heaving and moaning in her bedroom, thickening the silence of the hot summer afternoon. She rushed in, thinking someone was terribly sick. No one was sick inside, but her younger brother and husband were naked on the bed. Their muscular bodies glistened in the dark as they rocked rhythmically. She hadn't gone to the pond to take a long bath and cry that day. That red hibiscus tree was a sapling then and the stone was a little larger back then. She was too confused and shocked to know what was going on. So she couldn't cry. She ran back to the fields. A little while later, a very happy Horo was back, his short, white gamusa looped between his legs. She had noticed red teeth marks on one of his thighs and somehow stopped herself from crying aloud.

Anil was visibly happy too. She didn't ask him who he was because he could be anyone, and Anil could lie. She hadn't seen him before; Anil must have picked him up somewhere; maybe they studied together or worked together for the 'party'. She didn't care, and when Anil asked her for the third time if she was feeling sick and why she was in bed during the day, she lied that she had a headache. She knew he had expected her to boil some tea because there was a guest. Not with milk necessarily. He had wanted some black tea with sugar—not the usual tea with salt, which was what they had to make do with usually. The boy's voice was deep and sonorous. He had said they could have tea another day, perhaps at Tetelia market on their way to the bus stop.

Her husband's disease had ruined her life. Many nights she had spent burning beside him, sliding her finger between her legs and crying when she climaxed—not out of happiness but desperation, and hatred for her younger brother, who she had thought was closest to her and not to the man who had married her saying she was the most beautiful woman he had ever seen. Yes, she had eloped with him. High-caste brahmins were not allowed to marry anyone below their caste, and he belonged to the koch community, an indigenous community lower down the rung than brahmins.

They had spent several months in the house of one of his aunts in remote Hatimuria village, and returned to her village only after Anil was born. That aunt was no more. She had died a year after Anil brought a man to his room for the first time. He was twenty-nine then and hadn't yet graduated even after four attempts. Horo had died in an accident a couple of years ago, and she had married two of her three daughters off. A little after the counter-insurgency operations started, all the elders in the village advised her that, if she didn't get them settled soon, an Indian soldier might 'touch their bodies, and no boy in this world would be ready to marry them'. So, she hastily married them off to men twice their age. When the army raped four girls from their village and a woman six months pregnant, she thanked God she had listened to the elders.

She had noticed then that Anil wanted space and privacy. During meals, he would often say that he did not like to disturb her sleep when 'party meetings happened' in his room. Neerumoni hated those party meetings and so didn't want to release any funds for an extension to the house. She dreaded the meetings that made him flunk his college exams year after year until he grew such a thick moustache that he began feeling awkward about sitting in a classroom with slim, young boys and girls.

One thing she liked about Anil was that he handed over all the earnings from the fields every month and did not keep anything for himself. Every Sunday or Monday morning, he asked her for a few rupees to buy betel nut, tobacco, cigarettes, and she gave it to him without asking a question. After several months of implicit requests for money to expand the house, when she did not respond, he began to keep a little aside before handing her the rest. That had been the beginning of Anil having a space entirely for himself, she thought.

With the money, to weave the roof, he bought long straws fashioned from seron, which grew like wild grass on river banks, and cut fat bholuka bamboos from their backyard, where the red hibiscus bloomed and the shrinking black stone sat. And he built a single-room hut two feet away with a four hands-high earthen veranda. On the day he was shifting his things from the main house, he kept saying how good the new arrangement would be. He didn't look into her eyes, but spoke of how she would not wake up to the din of debates during party meetings, and that she would be able to sleep well and her blood pressure would not rise anymore. He left most of his childhood items—mainly books and some clothes from his younger days—in the main house. Later, when he said he was going to sleep and shut the door, she sat in his old room for a long time. She picked up a pair of old shorts and was filled with wonder at how tiny this man used to be. Then she laughed—of course he was tiny, he had come out her stomach after all. He was smaller, yes, he was.

No sounds came that night, but the next night she couldn't sleep. She stood near her son's door and listened to the sounds and, in the wee hours of the morning, when the bamboo door creaked, Neerumoni hid herself. Promod's fair skin was glowing; she knew him instantly. He was Nirgun's younger brother, around seven years younger than Anil. Nirgun was the leader of the party that contested elections against Anil's party.

People said, in a few years, Anil would become the village headman and everything would change for the family: there would be sugar to be had with tea, as many as seven to eight silk dresses and gold ornaments to wear, and meat every day. She only thought of duck meat when the village women said these things about her bright future. And when she thought of the ornaments, she would stare into the mirror, shocked at how she seemed uglier each time. She craved for the refection she used to see in the village pond during the days that Horo held her hand and said that she was the most beautiful woman in the world. Yes, she was. Of course she was. But after he acquired that disease and started pulling her own brother under his quilt in her absence, he didn't remain the passionate lover he once was. He would hold her desperately, push her petticoat up to her breasts and enter her. But she didn't like it that way. She had liked to be naked in his arms and to laugh and laugh, get tickled. She had wanted him to go down on her the way he used to before their marriage, on the wet sands near the village stream. Later, after their intense and passionate lovemaking, she used to sit naked there, the wet, sharp, sand grains pinching her butt, his limp penis stroking the side of her thigh as he dug his nose into her hair, her chest. He had long hair, like suntanned farmers used to in those days. Long hair that gave him a wayward look, like sturdy farmers who smelled like coconut water when they sweated while making love. But she came to associate that smell with her younger brother and her husband making love, because that night when she slept beside him, he didn't smell like that, it was the bed that smelled like coconut water.

*

Gurmail Singh, that burly Sikh soldier, was probably the one man that Anil loved. And she had seen him care deeply for her son. The army, which had moved out of the village, was back again that winter. A sense of fear spread through the village once again. There was no more sitting around a fire comfortably after dinner. Everyone went to bed early, and young men hid in the granaries, the forests and the hilly tracks all night.

The army didn't really care; they could kill anyone they found suspicious and no one would file a case against them. If someone did, their family's fate was sealed. The villagers knew it was better to run before the army began combing the village for separatist rebels. On one of those nights, while Anil and his mother were at dinner, they heard the sound of approaching boots. Their dog barked and, hearing him, all the dogs in the colony struck up a howl. It was eerie. The rest of the neighbourhood locked their doors and hushed their children. The smell of flowers and fresh cow dung floated in the air. Gurmail Singh and several other soldiers stood at their door. He must have been an officer, because the other soldiers stood at attention while he looked relaxed. Was there anyone else in the house, he asked, and when they said 'no', he didn't scream in Hindi like officers had done before. He called Neerumoni 'Mother' and asked for some water. While she was inside, getting him a glass of water, she felt him eye Anil suspiciously. Frightened and desperate, she started screaming in Assamese that her son was not a separatist rebel. Gurmail Singh told her to shut up.

He drank the glass of water she had brought him and pushed her son towards the outhouse, asking Anil to show him around and help him find anyone else hiding there. When she tried to go in, the other soldiers pointed the gun at her and asked her not to move. A while later, from the bedroom, she could hear Anil uttering a series of helpless, muffled no-nos and weeping like a child. It was evident from the grunts that he was trying not to scream. After a point, he let out a louder scream and then gradually his whimpers became sparse, before everything became silent. Neerumoni stood there and started to weep. She didn't want to scream and let the whole village know, because if they knew, Anil would turn into an object of ridicule.

Neerumoni didn't have the courage to go in after the soldiers left, but she could hear her son weeping in the silence of the night. When he careened out of the room with bowed head and walked towards the pond, she rushed in with the kerosene lamp and checked the bed.

The blood looked like a red rose blooming on the white bedsheet, and the room smelled like coconut water. Neerumoni sat there and cried. She wished Anil didn't have that pair of almond eyes with bow-shaped brows that allowed him to play Draupadi. People said he looked exactly like her, and when Anil as Draupadi cried during the public stripping scene in the village production, a lot of women in the audience took out their hankies.

They never spoke about it.

But that Gurmail Singh, who was responsible for the patch of blood on her white bedsheet, soon turned into Anil's love interest. He started to visit every other night and those same sounds invaded her sleep. She didn't understand how it happened, how her son ended up liking this hirsute man 'who had committed atrocities upon him'. The smell of coconut water kept chasing her and wouldn't let her sleep. She didn't want to ask him, nor could she tell anyone in the village. The army stayed for two years, and Anil was the happiest man in the village. Every month he went to different places, such as the hill stations Shillong and Halfong and Guwahati city, with Gurmail, and brought her different gifts. Villagers came to see Gurmail for suggestions and, for the first time, they were not scared of someone who worked for the Indian Army. He was, after all, one of them if he was their prospective village headman's closest friend. Yes, that rumour grew too—that Anil had great connections in the government through the tall army officer he was friends with, and it would be prudent to vote him to power instead of Nirgun, who was not very honest anyway. When Gurmail left, Anil cried a lot and so did Neerumoni, and so did several other villagers. The girls who had tied rakhi on his wrist and called him their brother came with beautifully patterned cotton gamusas and gifted them to him. Gurmail cried too and, three months later, when he came with his wife and two daughters, the whole village came out to meet him with more gifts, and Anil hosted them.

After staying away from Anil for several years, Promod started to visit again. She didn't know why exactly but Neerumoni knew that she disliked the boy. Somehow, she couldn't trust him—wasn't it his brother who had dared Anil to stand in the elections, declaring that he might lose his life if he did? Anil hadn't told her about it; she heard of the threat at the women's meeting in the village prayer hall. Leaving the rituals unfinished, Neerumoni rushed back home to wake up a sleeping Anil and ask him. He sounded peeved, and rebuked her for being so chickenhearted. She blurted out that he shouldn't be roaming around 'with that effeminate boy who had eaten the head of the beautiful wife he married, who committed suicide a month after their wedding'. Annoyed, Anil left in a huff. Promod would visit him at night and leave early in the morning when even crows were asleep in their nests.

That day, Anil left for the election campaign earlier than usual. They were going to campaign in the Maloybari area. Anil ate leftover rice with fresh green chillies and lime juice, and informed her he was leaving. She had felt sorry that he was eating such a frugal meal but, before she could say anything, he smiled and said that once he won the elections, things would change and they would eat meat every day. He was sure to win. Like any other day, after he left, she pushed open the door of his outhouse to clean it, but to her utter surprise, a stark-naked Promod was sleeping in the bed. Her blood boiled; the smell of coconut water made her crazy and she didn't know why, but she started to beat him with the broom, screaming and shouting 'Get out, get out', asking him if it wasn't enough that he had caused his wife's death. In the golden light of the early morning, the whole village saw a naked Promod running for his life, wheezing and howling. Anil came back late at night. He didn't have dinner. Mother and son had never spoken about what she thought of as his father's disease. So Promod's matter wasn't discussed either. In the middle of the night, she heard him crying. She felt sorry for what she had done.

But the damage was done. The whole village started to tease Promod, calling him 'Anil's wife'. Four days later, he was publicly humiliated by a band of men at the Tuesday Market. Promod went to his brother's room and swallowed a whole bottle of sleeping pills. In a furious rage, Nirgun went from house to house, telling them that Horo, the father, had suffered from 'that disease', and now the son was destroying the lives of younger men by dragging them to his bed. The village elders agreed. They said he should be taken to the sorcerer who could cure him, but Nirgun said he didn't 'believe in all that'. He would file a case. People should know the real character of the prospective head of the Village Council. On the fifteenth day after he took the pills, Promod was brought back from the hospital. A police officer took him straight to Anil's house, and asked if Anil was the person who had lured Promod into his room for a chat and then forced himself upon Promod.

A bewildered Neerumoni went from pillar to post after the arrest. Lots of reporters came, and were talking about something called 'Section 377' that could go in Anil's favour because it had just been repealed. Neerumoni noted down that number diligently on a piece of paper. She phoned Gurmail and told him to make a call on the number '377', because the kind reporter from Guwahati, who had come with a large camera and a strange car with a huge umbrella on top of it, and had coloured her eyelids blue, mentioned that it could be used to save her son. When Gurmail heard this, he began weeping. He wanted to say something but couldn't manage anything beyond the sentence that he would drop everything to come and help her. Things were sorted out when he came. Within two days. He made many calls on his mobile phone and urged Anil to call a Village Council meeting. Anil did not agree. He said, 'They will kill me.' Finally, Gurmail said he should stop behaving like a madman, and assured him that no one was against him or after his life. They thought it was just a disease, so Anil would just have to go and say that he would take good medical care once he became headman. They would then vote for him. Anil said he would withdraw his nomination papers. Nirgun's party was using every means to malign him. Reporters from the many local satellite channels might come back and make him out to be some sort of a demon. Gurmail said he had nothing to worry about, that he was with Anil and that he should fight the elections.

They ate meat that day. Duck meat. Gurmail had shopped, like in the days when he used to take Anil out for holidays in Shillong or Guwahati, and buy him new clothes; the days when he used to call Neerumoni 'Mother'. She slept well that night, even though the sounds invaded her ears and there was that coconut-water smell when she went to clean and arrange Anil's room. Neerumoni had cooked the duck meat with banana flowers and stir fried it with ginger and garlic paste. Gurmail said it tasted like the immortal nectar of the Gods, and she had laughed, blushed, laughed and laughed.

That night, when Anil went to pee in the backyard at midnight, someone tried to stab him with a sharp knife, but he raised an alarm and the knife only mangled the flesh on his arm. The whole village gathered as Neerumoni wailed and cursed, and Gurmail ran out with his gun to find who it was. He was shouting 'Come back, coward' in Hindi. An old woman from the village made a paste of marigold leaves and put a layer of it on Anil's wound. Someone found a fresh wad of cotton and tore some clean cloths into strips and bandaged him. The bleeding stopped. But it only made him more miserable.

Day after day, Anil slept. He showed no interest in the election campaigns and avoided repeated calls from senior party leaders in Guwahati. 'They will kill me,' he kept saying. The villagers murmured amongst themselves about what could be done. One evening, they began trickling into his courtyard. When the women saw that their men were going to visit Anil, they were curious. They said to each other, 'Why shouldn't we go too?' and 'Who knows, if we explain things to him, he may yet stand for the elections.' So they nodded at one another, combed their hair, slipped their bangles on, pushed betel nut with thin wads of tobacco into their mouths and followed their men. When the children started to follow, they said, 'Go away, we will be back soon.' But the children followed anyway. Perhaps they too sensed that something was about to happen.

That afternoon, in front of almost the whole village, Anil agreed that he would contest. Just then, a young man from the village came up to him and whispered that Nirgun had come to know about this meeting, and that his brother, Promod, was a few metres away, not daring to come closer. 'Promod is crying. He asks if you will ever forgive him. He says, "Ask him to stand for the elections and I will vote for him."' The man handed over to Anil a crumpled piece of paper on which was written, 'It was my brother who forced me to do all these things. I love you still.'

A strong smell of kerosene and petrol woke Anil up. He wondered why he was dreaming of weird smells when he was in the arms of the man he loved most. Anil brought the naked body of Gurmail closer and dug his nose deeper into his chest. He put his arms around Gurmail's waist. They had made love passionately after a long time and he was feeling happy-tired. The bed was wet with their sweat and he took a deep breath, taking it all into his lungs, and once again he smelled kerosene and petrol. 'Anil!' Gurmail was screaming at the top of his voice. He was pulling his pyjamas up and asking Anil to run. Anil didn't know what to do, and Gurmail only said, 'Just run! Get out!'

The house was on fire: the newspapers that had been collecting ever since he moved to the outhouse, the clothes, the almirah and the old wooden furniture: everything was on fire. Someone flung the door open. Anil had wrapped the bedsheet around his waist by then. It was his mother.

'They are trying to kill you,' she screamed. 'Someone set the house on fire and locked this door.'

He stood there, not knowing what to do, and it suddenly struck him that this could have killed his lover and his mother, and that it was all because of him. In the courtyard, he howled and cried, and Gurmail said, 'Shut up, it's not because of you. I am going to find who did it.' Neerumoni hugged Anil and cried. He clung to her and said that it was all because of him, that he shouldn't have agreed to contest the elections. He should have instead gone to the forest with Gurmail and never come back.

That was the first time he spoke to her about it, and they both looked at each other. His mother's back was to the house. It was burning down. He turned his eyes to the flames engulfing what had been home, for he couldn't look into her eyes anymore. He had built that house to carve a space of his own. It had implicitly told his mother what his 'male needs' were. And now, in front of the burning house, he was telling her that he loved Gurmail.

The fire had spread to the whole house now and his mother was howling, saying something he didn't understand. He released himself from Neerumoni's arms in a fleeting second and started running towards it. 'Leave it, leave! Life is bigger than the things you are trying to get!' Instinctively, she had cautioned him, but when he went in and latched the door from inside, she knew that he hadn't gone in to bring anything back. She wailed and clawed at the ground. Gurmail came back too late. He had gone in search of the person who had set fire to Anil's home. By this time, the whole neighbourhood had woken up to an unusual smell—burnt human flesh, the smell of burnt human flesh.

ल

LIKE THE THREAD IN A GARLAND

What Nishad suspected about Rubul before his wedding:
November 2016

My best friend Rubul—who is thirty-nine and still a virgin—married Anuradha on the fifth of November 2016. For a long time, I wondered whether he was gay. But, after close assessment over eighteen years, I have concluded that he is not. That's why, when people gossip about his sexuality, I am the one who denies it most vehemently. However, since our friendship is legendary, and his first girlfriend even spread the rumour that we were lovers, few believe me.

'He is not, I know him very well, he has been my best friend since we were kids.'

'Oh really,' they say.

We were seventeen when he was with his first girlfriend. I don't know why, but he froze when she grabbed him the night she came to stay over at his place. He sent her to sleep in his sister's room, and two days later she broke up with him. He was so depressed.

Anyway.

Those things happened almost two decades ago. There is another problem to tackle now. Rubul has now been married for four days and they haven't had sex because of his lack of initiative. He hasn't even kissed her. He held her hands several times. Squeezed them twice. Once, she walked into him changing. He smiled awkwardly and turned his back to her.

Anuradha is very upset. On the first night—the wedding night on the flower-bedecked bed, like in the movies—Anuradha pretended to be the coy bride. She had read in an Assamese women's magazine that men are aroused when women are shy and show mild resistance. But Rubul took her pretence seriously and froze. My guess is that he didn't want to be the guy who had only sex on his mind on the wedding night. So, when she gently removed his hand from her arm, Rubul wondered if she was tired. Because he was exhausted. The wedding rituals were draining. And he had fasted all day. He was allowed to eat only fruits and palm sugar with water for dinner. He wasn't sure what the rituals for women were like, but he was sure that it was much more arduous for them. So he sat still for a few minutes and then said, 'We should sleep.' He switched off the lights and went to sleep without changing. In the middle of the night, he went to the bathroom, stayed there for a very long time, and returned wearing his shorts and a half-sleeved thermal T-shirt. In the light blue hue of the night bulb, she observed his legs. When he was climbing on to the bed, she hoped he would make a move, maybe climb on top of her too. She took a deep breath and prepared herself for the moment. But he just turned on to his side, away from her, and fell asleep immediately. Anuradha wanted to slide her hands around his waist and then slip her right hand down to the band of his shorts. But she was worried that Rubul, who was such a good boy, wouldn't approve of her behaviour. She didn't get any sleep.

Since she didn't sleep well, Anuradha woke up with a headache that made her hate everyone in her new home, including the family dog Khekarkhaiti. The next day was horrible, and horribly long. She was dressed up by Rubul's mother and Subho, her sister-in-law, forced to wear make-up, lipstick and heavy jewellery, and she had to sit in the living room, where people came to 'see the new daughter-in-law'. She didn't want to wear make-up. In her job as a small-time TV actor, she had to wear it for as long as fourteen hours a day, and had since developed a deep aversion to applying anything on her face. She also didn't want to wear any more silk. Or jewellery. She had played a dutiful daughter-in-law in the TV series, wearing gaudy outfits even while shooting kitchen scenes. She wanted to wear shorts and her black T-shirt that said 'I AM NOT PAID TO BE NICE TO YOU' and watch soap operas that didn't make any sense. The day was long because she had to touch the feet of at least fifty-two people and smile at 192 people as part of post-wedding rituals. She decided whose feet to touch or not based on how much grey hair they had. A number of people asked her if she would complete her master's degree, advised her to be patient, and ninety-nine people whispered in her ears about having a baby soon because 'post twenty-five pregnancies were hard and wouldn't be good for the baby'. At a certain point, she felt that the silly role she played in the Assamese mega-serial wasn't entirely fictional. It was based on her life.

At the end of the day, she decided Rubul was the root of all her misery. At least she ought to have had good sex before that ordeal. She had been waiting for the wedding night for so long. Why did she go through that painful bikini wax if her new husband had no interest in her? After the marriage was fixed in May 2016, they often met alone in her house or in parks, where the possibility of making out was high. But he didn't make a pass. Occasionally, he held her hand and that sent ripples through her body, because he was so handsome and smelled so good. Like, manly. Manly without cologne. She thought, 'Oh, he respects me and doesn't want me to me feel like I am just a piece of ass, so he isn't staring at my boobs or placing his hand strategically on my thighs or letting his hand "accidentally" slip from the waist to my ass.' Those are the signs of a good boy—at least in Anuradha's referential universe. So she was convinced that, after they were married, he wouldn't sleep around with his co-workers. She didn't even consider the possibility that he might be gay. In her universe, gay men are effeminate, and worked as choreographers, fashion designers and make-up artists. So, five months after their wedding was arranged, she married him without having sex even once. And in the lead up to it, she spent her days imagining how he would rearrange her bones on the first night and how they would leave the bedroom like the scene of a battle.

Rubul hasn't told me any of that. And honestly, I really don't want to know. I know this because Anuradha is friends with Rishav: THE BOY I MET AT A PARTY AND MADE OUT WITH. But later I started dating his sister Pooja and am in a relationship with her now. And Rishav is very upset about that. But since he is still not out, he can't tell his sister about our episode. He remains in touch with me through rude messages that sound like banter but is not. Rishav is unhappy that I am dating his sister and not him. He dislikes me and he wants attention from me. Anyway, it is too late for that now. Pooja has met my parents and we are kind of semi-serious and partly monogamous.

Rishav texts, 'You are such an asshole, just like your best friend Rubul, who has destroyed Anuradha's life.'

I write back, 'It is not conclusively proven that Rubul is queer.'

'He doesn't fuck a beautiful girl like Anuradha, and you are saying he is not queer?'

'I need you to grow up. I can't be part of this conversation. We will talk again in ten years, when you are thirty-four. Bye.'

He will message me again in a few weeks and we will have a similarly rude conversation. His sister, Pooja, is four years younger than me, but she's over thirty and we can talk like adults.

Rishav is pissed. Really pissed.

Anyway, I was talking about Rubul. Anuradha is very annoyed right now. She would take a sledgehammer and break down a mountain if she could. She complains about her sexless marriage to Rishav all the time. Rishav, who is damn gossipy, tells Pooja everything. Poor Rubul's entire life is now stored in the form of encrypted messages on WhatsApp, and gleefully shared screenshots. Rubul has never spoken about his sex life with me. And he wouldn't have either unless it had become a serious problem. I knew that. But a week after the wedding, Rubul called me on FaceTime audio.

'I need to discuss something serious with you. When are you coming to Assam?'

'What? About your marriage?'

'Yes, how did you know?'

'Hahaha.' That's my way of ignoring the question.

'How did you know?'

'Hahaha.'

'Nishad, it is important.'

'Tell me what you want to discuss with me.'

'I have to meet you for that, but you are in Delhi and I am 2,000 miles away in Assam. You told me some things before the wedding. I should have listened to you.'

I sighed. 'You know I was just cautioning you! And I never wished for those things to come true.'

Rubul said something like yes-I-know. My heart sank. Once, when we were nineteen, and Rubul and I were lying on the edge of a pond after a long day of fishing, he had rolled over to me and pressed his lips against mine, sucking on them. I froze. I had not expected him to do that. We never talked about it because I did not kiss him back. When he was done, I said, 'We should get home.' The sky was bright blue. The crickets were singing relentlessly

*

A week after that conversation with Rubul (two weeks since his wedding), I rang him. 'Guess what? I got promoted.' He was overjoyed, and made some muffed excited sounds since he was still at work.

'I want to throw a small party during the last week of December at my new apartment. It will be a sort of housewarming too. This means we can talk. How are things between you and Anuradha? Are they better?'

'When you visit, I will talk to you.' Rubul's tone had changed.

'Rubul, you aren't postponing dealing with a serious problem, right?'

I think he sensed the urgency in my low voice. I don't lower my voice usually. Nor do I speak that slowly. He could hear caution and worry in my voice, and if I was worried enough, he knew I would have a chat with his mother. Though we are exactly the same age, I was always the big brother, approving things, sorting stuff out for him. He knew that. I would find out later that he didn't want it. That he was postponing dealing with a serious problem.

But that day, he just said, 'I won't do anything without telling you. See you soon.'

'That means you are planning to do something.'

'Yes.'

God, is he going to come out? I started to sweat at the thought of it.

What Nishad told Rubul Before Getting Married:
May 2016

First, you really need to know more about this girl. That she lives in Azara, has a degree in history and respects elders is not enough information on which you can decide to get married to someone … Rubul, you don't get married because it will bring joy to the family. You get married because you want to get married. So what if she is chosen by your mother? Does your mother know you drink nowadays? That you have graduated from rum to whisky during social occasions, and that you have also eaten pork and betrayed your brahmin caste? So what if she is chosen by your mother? With all due respect to Babita Aunty, she doesn't know what you want. You want a partner, Rubul. You want someone with whom you can sit down and discuss your favourite movie, favourite novel. After you write a scene for one of those stupid television serials, you want someone who knows you well enough to comment on it and push you to work harder … Wait, you misunderstand me. I am not asking you not to marry Anuradha. I mean, she sounds lovely and, from that photograph you showed me, I see she is pretty. But that's not enough reason to marry a girl. You marry because you want to marry this person and no one else. I mean, just tell your mother that you don't want to commit to a wedding now, and at least hang out with her for the next six months before you decide to marry her.

Wait, what? What do you mean, she isn't that type of girl? Which world do you live in? I am not even asking you to have sex with her. Just go out. What? Is her family putting pressure? But she is only, like, what, twenty-five? There is something fishy here. Can you find out why they are pressing your family to decide within a week? Does she know that you come home very late at night? That you work for twelve hours, fourteen hours? Your mother, sister, father may stand for it. But why would she tolerate that? You will have to now return home early. You will have to make sure her needs are met. You can't just return home at two in the morning, ask for dinner to be heated and then go sleep. You will have to chat with her, make love to her. Marriage is a responsibility. She will be waiting for you all day. Especially because she doesn't have a job right now.

What are you going to do? In your own words, this is something you can't change about yourself. Have you told her? Okay, you haven't. Why haven't you told her? When you are marrying her, you are taking responsibility for her. You can't expect her to tolerate everything that you do like your mother and sister. Can you?

OMG, she has a boyfriend who is threatening her and telling her not to marry you? Okay, this is serious! If you don't tell Aunty, I will call her. What if he harms you? What if he tries to attack you? I am terrified of these surrendered insurgents. If he is a former militant, he must be like fifty? Okay, fine, forty. So what? They still roam around the state with a gun and they don't think before using it. They have lots of money, ya. I am terrified. Of course, I am! Will you go argue with someone who is carrying a gun? You know how it is! You know that no one can actually control former militants. And seriously, and this is my final point, what if she votes for Modi?'

What Babita told Nishad after the wedding date was decided:
June 2016

Nishad, the first thing Anuradha did when she entered our house was to look at Rubul's grandfather's photo— my father-in-law, who was a freedom fighter and such a wonderful person. Then she joined her hands in salutation to him, and it was at that moment I knew that I had made the right choice. Also, you know, that morning, I went inside the prayer room, lit a ghee lamp, shut my eyes and prayed, 'God, the girl is stepping into this house for the first time today since the wedding date was fixed. I have sprinkled holy water everywhere and have also asked the maid to mop the entire house with salt water to neutralise the power of evil spirits, but now it is in your hands. You have to show me a sign. You have to.' Then, you know what happened, Nishad? I felt a gust of wind. I felt as if someone entered the prayer room! One of the red hibiscus flowers tucked into the hands of the statue fell on my lap. I was worried that the wind had put out the lamp, but when I opened my eyes, the wick was burning bright, the fame was strong and the room felt warm. It was a very strong flame.

Tell me Nishad, do togor flowers bloom in June? We have that large togor flower in the courtyard, remember? When it blooms in April, the smell travels almost to the main road. Everyone talks about our togor flower. On very rare occasions, it blooms in May too. But that morning, I saw a lonely togor flower. It was surreal. But I knew it was a message. I knew I had chosen the right girl for my son, that it is the ideal match.

You are family, so there's nothing to hide from you. You know that Rubul's sister will now move to the top floor since he is getting married? I mean, we middle-class people plan everything, don't we? She wasn't in my plan. I didn't plan to build a top floor. The foundation of this house is for four doors, but I thought, later, when Rubul earns, he will build as per his requirements. But his sister's marriage didn't work. She had to return to us. Now, when Rubul's bride comes home, there will be space constraints. I mean, we will manage, but there will be some discomfort, right? So I have asked Subho to move upstairs. She will put a part of that floor on rent, and live alone with her two children. Cook on her own. Live independently. I don't want the two girls to have tussles. When Anuradha heard that, she became so sad. She asked, can't she stay downstairs, with us? Note that she said 'with us'. She held Subho's hand and said, 'Please don't go. People in the colony will think I am a horrible person who made sure her sister-in-law is driven out of the first floor even before she stepped into the house as a bride. What will they say about me?' You know, Nishad, this cemented my belief: this is the kind of girl I want for my son and she is just like the character she plays in the serial. This is why, though she is a supporting actress, people love her. In the serial, she is like the moral core of the story that is full of horrible, scheming mothers-in-law and sisters-in-law. But in reality, too, she is pure like water from the Ganga. And in our house, too, she will be the moral and ethical core. She will come and keep the house together like a thread in a garland. She won't let things fall apart. She will be the foundation of the house. She will be like a lamp and spread light in the house.

What happened when Nishad invited Rubul and his family to lunch:

December 2016

I had thrown the lunch party to celebrate my promotion, but it was also a sort of housewarming since I had bought this apartment six months ago and did nothing to mark its possession. All the guests were invited to come by 1 p.m., but I had asked Rubul and his family to arrive by noon. I knew Rubul would delay by an hour—that was standard. So I lied to Rubul, 'I have asked all the guests to be here by noon, so you can come no later than 1.' I knew Rubul knew that I was lying. 'And listen, we will find a spot to talk about your problem.

'Don't worry about it. I was getting fed up. So I took care of it and now things should be fine.' Rubul sighed. It wasn't really a sigh of relief, so I was surprised and still curious.

'Are you sure? What did you do?'

'No one can be sure. I will tell you everything when we meet. Do you remember Vikas from our batch?'

'Vikas Surana? The doctor? Yes, I do. I didn't know you were friends with him. He used to bully everyone.'

'Yes, but now he doesn't bully anyone. He helped me.'

Vikas was an oncologist. He wasn't a psychiatrist. My mind raced. Was Rubul suffering from erectile dysfunction, did Vikas prescribe drugs? I couldn't wait to meet him the next day and take him aside for a proper chat. He should see an expert. Not a friend who is a doctor.

At three in the afternoon, Rubul and his family still hadn't turned up. Bina-pehi, my aunt, who was supervising the caterers, asked me what to do. The caterers were anxious to leave; they had more or less packed up, and Rubul's family were the only guests still to arrive.

I looked outside; the weak winter sun would probably set in less than an hour. I suggested that we could store whatever was left in casseroles, including Rubul's favourite, the chicken liver.

At four, I called Rubul for the third time and it went unanswered. Finally, I called Babita Aunty.

She said, 'I guess you know it is not my fault.'

'Yes, I know. Rubul hasn't turned up to pick you guys up, right?'

'Yes. I am still dressed. The new bride is watching TV. We are all waiting.'

'How surprising.'

'Subho is pissed and won't talk to him, so I am calling every half an hour like a maniac, and your best friend won't even receive my calls.' She was clearly very annoyed.

'Well, Subho's resolve won't last long, will it?' I heard her sigh at the other end. 'Did you tell your new daughter in-law that this is standard behaviour for Rubul?'

'Don't ask. What can I say? We could have rented a cab, but he said he would come on time to pick us up.'

'Well, the poor girl must be dying of hunger.'

'I think I will just steam some rice and we will have it with leftover dal. We didn't cook lunch today because we were to eat at your place. We will come, baba. We will come. Maybe we will turn up in an hour and have an early dinner.'

I rang again, an hour later. My apartment was now empty. The guests and the caterers had left. My parents had also left for their own house on the outskirts of the city. Bina-pehi decided to stay back so she could help me just in case Rubul & Co. made a late-night appearance.

Rubul's mother said, 'He is still stuck somewhere. So early dinner plan cancelled. We will have dinner with you. Heat up the leftovers and we will have them at dinner time. Subho ate some fruits and cornflakes. Anuradha and I were so hungry, we just ate some rice with dal. The poor girl was all dressed up. She has changed into sweatpants now.'

We both laughed. 'If your son doesn't change his ways, your new bride will go running back to her mother's house, you know that, right? And no God can stop her.'

'I know.' She sighed. 'I thought he would change after marriage.'

I hung up and looked at the orange sky, the homecoming birds. From the fourth floor, you couldn't see the dirt, the manhole, the mud puddles on the road. From the fourth floor, you could see the round shape of the mosque clearly and the parking lot of this apartment complex. At night, halogen lights lit up the area. Rubul won't change, I knew. I also knew that this would cost him his marriage.

They turned up at 11 p.m. I was watching something on Netflix, trying hard to stay awake.

'We are heeeerrreee!' Rubul screamed from the parking lot. It was too cheerful, and very annoying. I walked slowly to the balcony and saw him waving at me. Babita Aunty, Anuradha and Subho looked sullen.

'We are in time for linner!!' he announced as he stepped out of the elevator.

That was hardly likely to bring anyone cheer. But Subho managed a smile at me as she handed me a box of cashew sweets. Anuradha looked exhausted when she greeted me.

'We are on time for linner!' Rubul repeated in the same cheerful tone, since no one had responded to his announcement.

'Rubul, don't try to be funny,' I said.

'Do you even know what linner means? I invented the word yesterday. It is short for Late Dinner.' He looked at everyone, as if for an applause.

'Rubul, don't try to be funny,' Subho said and walked into the apartment. She saw Bina-pehi and, even before hugging her, started to complain about her brother.

'My family loves bitching about me,' Rubul said with a grin on his face.

'They have every reason to,' I replied.

'Exactly, Nishad-da,' Anuradha said.

Rubul just grinned.

I was sleepy, tired and angry, but I felt sorry for Anuradha—it had been a frustrating marriage for her. She had bought a new mekhela–sador for this occasion. She was also looking forward to meeting my parents for the first time since the wedding, and had also bought gifts for them. During dinner, she was mostly quiet.

The apartment complex was quiet, and with no one around but the guards on duty outside, it was unbearably silent. I put on some music by Zubeen Garg: 'Mayabini ratir bukut'.

'I will just have plain rice with dal,' Anuradha said when my aunt started to serve her.

On the table, there were brinjal fritters, chicken cooked with cashew paste, fish in a tomato curry soured with a lemon, goat rogan josh, sautéed cauliflower and potatoes, and palm jaggery kheer and shiny light-brown lalmohans for dessert. So, of course Bina-pehi's eyes popped in horror.

'Why? Why don't you want to eat? You think we don't cook well?'

'No, no, not at all.' Anuradha shook her head vigorously.

'Do you think our kitchen is dirty?' 'No, no, what are you saying?' she gasped.

'I have no doubt your mother cooks better than this, but does that mean you will go hungry in our house? I am sad.'

'No, no, please don't be sad.' Anuradha looked like she would burst into tears.

'We know the caterers for a very long time. They are clean and they make healthy food, Anuradha.' My aunt continued to hurl missiles at the poor girl.

This is the tactic the host uses to guilt-trip guests into overeating: nine pieces of chicken instead of three, an extra bowl of kheer, four slices of cake instead of one and, of course, a lot of rice—like, a lot. That the new bride who was visiting for the first time would eat only rice and dal was an alarming situation for my aunt. That's why she pulled out her most powerful weapons at the very beginning.

Anuradha, who was speaking softly so far, protested loudly, 'No, no, that's not the case.' She looked towards me for support, for reasons I will never know. 'I have heartburn,' she muttered.

'It is okay.' I came to her rescue. 'Let her eat what she wants. She ate a late lunch today, why won't she have indigestion and heartburn?'

Subho praised the chicken. 'The chicken is just amazing. Anuradha, you sure you don't want a little?'

'I am sure.'

My aunt continued to lament. 'You are the chief guest of today's lunch, Anuradha! You have to eat something. I will be so sad if you don't eat. Are you alright? Can I get you some Pudin Hara or Hajmola for your heartburn? I also have trifala—when we had heartburn, Ma used to feed us trifala. Now I am worried about you, my dear.' Bina-pehi's voice grew louder with every sentence.

I was sure Anuradha was fine. And that she didn't have heartburn, or if she did, it wasn't serious. She was launching a passive resistance against her irresponsible new husband turning up eleven hours late for a meal they were invited to.

'I am fine. I don't want anyone to worry about me,' she repeated, staring at her plate.

Rubul also knew what was going on. And perhaps his mother and Subho, too. He took the ladle, picked up a leg piece with a generous helping of cashew gravy. 'We will worry about you. And I will, of course, worry about you.' Then he poured it over her rice.

Anuradha was startled. She wasn't prepared for that. She paused. Then she slowly pushed her unfinished plate of food towards the centre of the table—just a few inches. I was surprised she didn't raise her voice or push her plate away with more force.

'I am done.'

'You won't eat the chicken I served you?' Rubul asked. As if rejecting the chicken piece he served meant that she was rejecting him.

She looked straight into his eyes and said coldly, 'No. I said I have heartburn.'

He looked at her for a few seconds. It was so awkward. Then he looked down at his plate and took a spoonful of rice and meat to his mouth. I knew he would do something stupid, but I didn't know he would do something so stupid. I saw his eyes turning red. Suddenly, he pushed his plate away to the centre of the table. It collided with a glass of water that fell on the table and spilt over on to Anuradha's clothes. Then he stormed out of the dining room. 'No need, no need to eat.' First, he said that in a muffed tone and, when he had taken about four steps, he said it loudly. 'NO NEED, NO NEED TO EAT.'

Anuradha started to shed tears. 'How is any of this my fault? I said I won't eat chicken and he is forcing me to eat.'

I looked at everyone and said, 'I am not going to talk to Rubul. He is misbehaving.'

'No, you should give him two tight slaps,' Babita Aunty said.

*

Five minutes later, I was thrusting a plate of fried chicken liver at him. We were standing on the balcony. It wasn't too cold. We both wore light sweaters. I asked him what was wrong with him, and he said he had work to do. What did he want to talk to me about a month ago, I asked, and he said this wasn't the best time. I told him he couldn't be eleven hours late, and he couldn't stall people who were waiting for him by assuring them that he would be there to pick them up in an hour, in two hours, in half an hour. They could have taken an Uber if he had let them leave the house, but he stalled them for eleven hours. That wasn't acceptable. He said, no one understood him, and I laughed. I ate the chicken liver fry, laughed, and said that there was nothing to understand, that he was being an asshole.

He looked into my eyes and said, 'You have no idea what I am going through, Nishad.'

'What do you mean? You said you took care of the problem.'

'I thought I did, but I don't think I will be able to solve the problem. It is not under my control.'

'And Vikas? You said he helped you.'

'He did, but he can't make the problem go away.'

I could come up with a list of therapists I trusted, but it would take a lot of effort to persuade someone like Rubul to visit one. Still, I would have to do it. Rubul would start with 'I am not mad, I don't need a therapist', and I was ready to talk him out of those misconceptions.

So I said, 'Listen, what is it? Let me help you.'

'I don't want to trouble you or put you in any danger.'

'Danger? What kind of danger?'

It seemed to me Rubul wanted to avoid the topic, and I wanted to say, there was no danger. If he wanted to get out of the marriage even now, I would help him, talk to everyone. One didn't have to remain trapped in a loveless, sexless marriage.

'You have to tell me now. What danger?'

Rubul covered his face with his hands. 'I should have listened to you, Nishad. You always had a sense. You always knew better. You know me better than me. And your gut feeling about people and situations is usually correct.'

'You are scaring me now.'

'I will come tomorrow morning. I need to discuss this problem with you. I can't start here. I don't want Ma and Anuradha to know.'

'Of course. Come for breakfast tomorrow,' I said.

Inside, the atmosphere had turned cheerful. Anuradha was not weeping anymore. She was talking about recipes with Bina-pehi, and Subho was switching channels and commenting on dresses and make-up. Babita Aunty gave him a look, but I gestured to say 'not now'.

A little later, Rubul cracked terrible jokes at which only Anuradha laughed, Subho pretended to laugh, his mother didn't laugh, and a totally unresponsive Bina-pehi looked confused and sleepy—as if she was joke proof. A couple of hours later, I watched them walk to the car from the fourth-floor balcony. I wanted to go downstairs to see them off, but they all insisted I stay home since it was cold and quite late. But it was cold on the balcony, too. I watched Anuradha holding Babita Aunty's hand, helping her get in the car though she didn't need any help; Subho still yawning, chattering; and Rubul walking towards the car to unlock the doors. Just then, a tall, bearded man in a black leather jacket came as if from nowhere and punched Rubul. He was holding a gun. Before Rubul could make sense of what was going on, the man pressed the pistol against his temple.

*

Was it a revolver? Was it a pistol? What was it? I had no idea! For a few seconds, I froze. I had grown up in Assam during the worst years of violence; I grew up reading all those reports about people getting killed, civilians being armed, the killings between rival groups, former insurgents killing underground ones. But I had never actually seen any of it. Despite growing up in a state full of violent insurgent movements, I had never touched a gun. So I just froze; it was like I was watching a film.

The bearded man was drunk, perhaps. Still holding the gun to Rubul's head, he said something. Rubul appeared to reply, fear writ large on his face. He looked different without his spectacles. The man looked angry and was shouting. He was broad, had a large head and his unzipped jacket revealed a blood-red T-shirt. He wore a gold chain that shone in the light of the halogen bulbs. And then it really became like a movie, like one of those Hindi movies. Anuradha pushed Rubul aside, pounced on the man, snatched his gun and held it to her own forehead, just between her thick bow shaped eyebrows. In the quiet night, I heard her voice loud and clear, 'If you don't leave right away, I will shoot myself.'

The man started to shake his head. Perhaps he was saying, no, no. Still shaking his head, he crumpled to the ground and started to cry, 'Don't do that.' His voice was loud, and pierced through the silence of the night.

It was then that I came back to my senses, grabbed my phone and went downstairs. I guessed that Anuradha knew the man from before. They were close. Very close.

When I reached the parking lot, Babita Aunty was throwing up, and Rubul was trying to make her drink some water. I wanted to say something but couldn't think what.

The bearded man was gone.

Anuradha screamed, the gun still in her hands, 'We have to leave. He may come back with his friends. He is crazy.'

'What? Why didn't you say that earlier?' Babita Aunty screamed as she sprung up and slid into the car. 'Kill me-o! Just kill me here-o!' she cried.

Rubul was dazed and shocked, and in no position to drive. I pushed him inside the car and asked Anuradha to sit next to me. 'We can't go home. He knows Rubul's address,' she said, pointing the gun towards the road.

'I know where to go. Give me the keys,' I said.

'Kill me-o! What are you showing me, God? Anuradha, why are you still holding the gun? What if—'

'Don't worry, Ma, I know how to use a gun.'

Suddenly, there was an awkward silence. We stared at Anuradha for a few seconds, slightly scared.

Babita Aunty broke that silence, 'Oh god, my daughter in-law knows how to use a gun, and I thought those hands will nurture everyone and everything in my house. My gun wielding daughter-in-law! My son hasn't seen a gun in his life! Even I haven't touched a gun in my life, and I have a daughter-in-law who knows how to use a gun.

'Ma, please shut up,' Rubul snapped.

'Kill me, kill me now,' Babita Aunty said, looking at Anuradha.

'Drive! Now!' Anuradha said to me, calmly, the gun still in her hand.

At that point, I wanted to talk to Babita Aunty about some flower that bloomed out of season and gave her a sign, about flowers that fell on her lap, about the perils of hurriedly arranging a wedding, about pushing her own son and family down the slippery slope of a forced marriage.

But I didn't say any of that because I was suddenly full of admiration for Anuradha's courage. How she had taken stock of the situation, like a lifeguard on a beach! How she was giving me directions in a calm, resolute voice! When I told her that we would take refuge in my parents' house, she said she knew another way. She knew secret roads to my own parents' house that I didn't know. The house where I had grown up, the house where Rubul and I had spent a good part of our childhood! The road she took was dark, potholed and narrow, but safe. She said the bearded man's large Scorpio would avoid such roads. Anuradha clearly knew this man well. She knew the model of his car, could predict his behaviour, knew how to use his gun and the roads he would avoid because he loved his car. What else did she know about him? His business enterprises? The length of his beard? The smell of his breath? Which molar caused him pain if he ate ice cream? The length of his penis? She knew him too well and it didn't bode well for her.

But I didn't care because, in less than half an hour, the secret road she had taken would land us at my parents' place, and they would be shocked to see us. Babita Aunty and my mother would cry thinking about what could have happened. Rubul could have been shot. I could have been shot. Everyone could have been shot. That same night, at some point, Rubul's mother would go up to Anuradha, still holding the gun, and slap her hard. 'I thought you would light up my house, but you are all set to burn it down!' She would tell Anuradha to pack up and leave the next day and, for the first time in his life, Rubul would disobey his mother. He would say that she saved his life and she wasn't going anywhere. Anuradha would weep silently, rubbing her face with her free hand, and Babita Aunty would hold my mother's hands and wail, 'The witch has already started to control my son.' I would give each of them a pack of tissues. Cry, cry your heart out, I would murmur. In a bit, everyone would stop crying. We would take action to ensure everyone's safety. At dawn, we would call Vikas Surana's father, a high-ranking police officer, because Vikas Surana, the school bully, the oncologist, had given Rubul his father's personal mobile number a few weeks ago. Mr Surana would assure Rubul that the man would be arrested. Anuradha would take the phone and provide every detail of the bearded man: his two residences, four phone numbers, names of his aides, his best friends and their numbers and addresses, possible hiding places, etc. 'Mr Surana, I have his gun as proof—yes, it is a .22 calibre revolver. Yes, he is a former militant,' she would add before placing the phone on the cradle.

'The witch knows everything, she might as well be married to him,' Babita Aunty would tell my mother, and my mother would look confused and ask her to hush.

But those things would happen later at night, between now and dawn. At this point, while driving the car, I am just full of admiration for Anuradha. She would be a good partner. Like the thread in a garland, she could stitch things together.

*

It is dawn.

I wake up Ramen-da, the help, and ask him to make tea for everyone. When the tea is brought out with a tray of Britannia thin arrowroot biscuits, Rubul picks up a cup and asks me to follow him upstairs. I am still processing the incidents of the night before. I am wondering what will happen to Rubul's marriage now. I am still full of admiration for Anuradha — her deft handling of the situation, the ability to decide on the spot ... When I make no move to follow, Rubul moves towards the stairs and asks again, 'Are you coming?'

He knows this house well. My room is upstairs. There are several photos of the two of us together framed and hung on the walls of that room. Photos from my birthday celebrations. Photos from the last day of our higher secondary with pineapple pastry smeared on our faces. We are in school uniforms. Grey pants. Red sweaters. Stork-white shirts.

'I think you should talk to Anuradha,' I tell him.

'I want to talk to you. NOW,' Rubul bellows.

Anuradha looks up at him. She is drinking tea, sitting a little away from Babita Aunty.

I have rarely seen Rubul this assertive. I realise he is very serious. I follow quietly.

'Shut the door.'

I do as asked, and sit on the bed. 'Tell me. But I think you should be talking to Anuradha. She is in a very difficult situation.'

'Fuck you, Nishad.'

'Fuck you.'

There is an awkward pause.

'This was the fucking problem I wanted to discuss with you. I have been receiving threats from her ex ever since the wedding date was fixed. I haven't told Anuradha about it. I didn't want to scare her.' Rubul was staring at the floor. 'I am so stressed that nothing has happened between us till now — you know what I mean?'

'Yes, I do.' I add with a smirk, 'You don't have to elaborate.'

'Fuck you.'

I sit next to him. 'She is your life partner. This is a decision both of you have taken together — to be together. You need to discuss everything with her. And after today, I have to tell you that she seems like someone who can really take charge. She might be younger than us, but she is damn smart. If you want to be with her, stop treating her like a child. She is your equal.'

'Yeah—I figured. Our honeymoon is next month. Maybe it will be a fresh start.'

I look at Rubul for a few seconds and say, 'Yes, don't return a virgin from your honeymoon.'

Rubul covers his face and laughs. He asks if he can confess something, then pauses, a smile on his lips. He shrugs, and then says that he doesn't like my new apartment, he likes this room, this house; it has character. I feel a strange sense of calm. I am not upset that Rubul doesn't like my new apartment. Perhaps I knew it already. So I agree. I tell him that I too miss this house. Rubul asks if that mango tree is still there, the one he climbed once to pluck mangoes and fell from, fracturing his left hand. Yes, that mango tree is still around. It continues to produce lots of fruits every summer. I miss this house, Rubul murmurs, his eyes shut. In a few seconds, he is in deep sleep.

I throw a light blanket on him and step out of the room. As I walk down the stairs, I hear Babita Aunty yelling at Anuradha. I hurry down. Rubul's door is shut. He won't wake up for a while.

আ

AFTER ANTHROPOLOGY

A DAY BEFORE they left for Matt's father's house in Sioux Falls, Raj cheated on Matt with a colleague. It was nothing more than a fleeting thing. But he thought it was important to tell Matt. He didn't cheat on Matt just to confess, but once he decided to ask Matt for a break in the relationship, Raj was filled with guilt and a strange sense of relief.

So, when Matt returned from work that night, Raj opened the door and looked at him pleadingly. 'I got a blowjob today,' he said, after Matt had taken a shower and changed, and then come to the kitchen to get a drink of water. Matt looked so bright and fresh. His hair was still wet. He didn't choke on the bottle of water, like you see in television soaps. He stopped drinking, placed the bottle on the kitchen counter and said, 'What the—?'

'Yes,' Raj said, turning his back to Matt, his heart beating fast.

Matt sat down on the couch, near Raj, and switched on the television. He lowered the volume. 'Who was it?' He was calm. His voice was lower than the lowered volume of the television; not the voice of a man whose partner had just told him that he cheated on him.

'Jim works with me at the restaurant. He's a waiter.'

'Is he hot? I've never seen him,' Matt said. They prepared dinner in silence. Raj wanted to cook rajma (Matt called them kidney beans) with ginger-garlic paste but did not have the energy for it. He thought Matt's reaction was strange.

They had been together for four years and this was the first time something like this had happened. In the early weeks and months of their relationship, when Matt checked out guys in malls, restaurants, on the sidewalks, Raj would be offended. He would ask Matt to 'rein your eyes' and walk around swollen-faced. Matt would smile indulgently, ask him not to worry, tell him that no one would snatch him away. Sometimes, he would run a finger along Raj's arm, from elbow to wrist, arousing him. But those were the early days.

'You're not angry?' Raj asked, breaking the silence. He hadn't eaten much.

'I'm glad you got a blowjob. Blowjobs are great.'

Raj looked at Matt with glassy eyes. He wondered why Matt had used the word twice, if not to stress on it.

'You're being sarcastic. I thought I should tell you. I like honesty.'

'So do I. I appreciate you telling me.'

Raj didn't understand how Matt could use the word 'appreciate' in this context. Matt appreciated many things: a lift to the grocery store, if someone brought him a new client, the recommendation of a good doctor or the friend who pet-sat when Matt and Raj were away in India for their holiday. But was it appropriate to use that same expression when your boyfriend tells you that he got a blowjob from someone else? After a while, when Raj was tossing the dishes into the dishwasher, Matt hugged him from behind, pressed his body against his, and said, 'I love you. It's okay. I'm not one of those husbands who would throw a ft. You made a mistake. You're sorry, that's why you told me. Let's forget about it.'

Raj wanted to say that he hadn't yet said sorry, and it was preposterous of Matt to assume it.

'I am not sure if I would react the same way if you fucked someone.'

'I know. And that is why I would never do it, baby.'

Raj didn't like the sound of 'baby' in Matt's voice that night. He felt as if Matt was mocking him. The high moral ground that Matt always took annoyed Raj. He was annoyed by how Matt laid stress on the 'I' in I would never do that, baby.

So he asked, 'What are you trying to say, really? Something happened today. I just didn't have control over what I wanted.' Raj was surprised that he wanted to scream at Matt, he wanted to ask: why are you being so nice, are you trying to make me feel worse?

'No, baby,' Matt said, irritating Raj further. 'I am trying to say that I know you love me, and only me, and nothing will change that. This encounter had no meaning. I'm not pleased with what happened, but it's okay. It happens. We should look at the larger picture.'

Matt had this theory: the Larger Picture Theory. He always looked at the larger picture and encouraged others to do it as well. He framed his larger-picture funda in such a manner that everyone else sounded foolish and short-sighted. He was the one who could look ahead. Had foresight. Was more tolerant. Accepting. The one who forgave all. And Raj felt he was always the guilty one, the foolish one, the smaller one, the less loving one. Matt's righteousness burnt through Raj.

That night, they slept far apart on their large bed. Raj wanted Matt to get angry. He thought about the hours of guilt he had suffered after the incident in the restroom and felt foolish. And he wondered whether Matt didn't pick a fight about it because he loved Raj less intensely now, or because they were planning to go to meet Matt's father for the first time. Minnesota had just passed the Marriage Equality Act after a bitter fight against the 'Vote No' campaign, and they had married in a small ceremony that some of their friends and none of their family attended. Matt's mother died long ago and his sister Kristine had left the house when she was fourteen. Raj's parents had stopped receiving his calls after he told them that he was marrying a man. Over the past few years, Matt and his father had renewed their relationship. 'After all, he's my father,' Matt says. 'My biological father.' I understand, Raj had said. Bloodline, family — words no one could understand better than an Indian. Indians are obsessed with those things, he would say. In fact, when Tony emailed two months ago, when Raj wasn't even thinking about the possibility of taking a break, it was he who had suggested that Matt accept the invite. He is your only family now, he told Matt, who was swinging like a pendulum between accepting and turning down the invite.

Though Tony had thrown Matt out of the house after finding him blowing the jumpsuit-clad plumber, he was still Matt's father, Raj said. Establishing an easy equation with his father could only liberate him, Raj added, deftly exploiting Matt's 'Larger Picture Theory'. But it was also true that Matt wanted his father's love and approval — not unusual for someone who had lost his mother when he was five and had only hazy memories of her. Secretly (and Raj knew this), Matt was still grateful that his father never married again, and made Matt his priority until he found out his son was gay in the least ideal way ever. In short, it was a complicated relationship, with layers of love and hate; you get a bit or more of both, irrespective of wherever you dig.

Later at night, Raj felt Matt's right hand on his shoulder. ' — wake?' he muttered. Raj didn't reply. He pretended he was asleep though he knew that Matt always knew when he was still awake. He wished Matt was a little petty, and wondered if he was so kind and generous and correct because Raj was different. But they had planned the trip to Sioux Falls two months ago, and it would now be terrible if he backed off. Maybe they could take a break from the relationship after the trip, he thought, before falling asleep.

*

On their way to Sioux Falls, they stopped at a small restaurant by the freeway to eat lunch. Matt ordered his salad with a lot of lettuce and Raj had a chicken burrito with a lot of sour cream. They ate in silence.

'Is something wrong?'

For a few seconds, Raj was silent and then decided to speak up, 'You know, okay, I'll just say it—I thought you were unnecessarily crabby this morning. Is it because of what I told you?'

Matt threw his hands up, exasperated. 'What is wrrrooooong with you? You're still thinking about it?'

'Then what is it?' Raj raised his voice but quickly realised he had created a scene.

They ate the rest of their lunch quietly. Raj wanted to ask Matt why he was so angry in the morning that the phones were not charged and the power banks not packed. They could charge their phones in the car and they would definitely make their way to his father's house without a GPS. Raj had dated Matt in the 'pre-smartphone days', and knew he was good with routes. He didn't say it, though, because he knew what Matt would say: 'When my phone dies, it drives me nuts.' Among the many things Raj had not figured out about Matt was what drove him 'nuts' and what didn't. Matt had a long of list of things that drove him nuts: a bad day at work, saltless steak, salad without lettuce, a dead phone, poor connectivity while travelling, unwashed underwear, used towels, flattened toothpaste tubes, too much snow in winter, too little snow in winter, salad with too much lettuce, internet outage and much else. Raj wanted to list it all, but he kept quiet. He didn't want to escalate the matter.

'There's something I need to tell you,' Matt said about an hour later, as he drove.

'You got a blowjob? Then we are even.' Raj was immediately ashamed about the sarcasm. In this way, their relationship would turn into an emotionally abusive one. 'Alright, tell me. I am sorry.'

'My father is a bit strange.'

'I guess he is. He disowned you and then owned you back when you became a lawyer. Very convenient.'

'No, I mean, he watches Fox News all day and drinks beer and eats only steak and, of course, he votes for the Republican Party. You might find it difficult to deal with him and I think he is a bit racist.'

Raj laughed for the first time in three days. 'I'm sure it will be fine. I've dealt with many racist people in this country! I don't care what he eats or who he votes for, but it is a bit worrying that he watches Fox News!'

'I'm serious … I'm a little worried, Raj.'

'It will be fine.'

'I'm going to meet my conservative father with my husband who conservative father is introducing me to his fiancée. I mean, all those years after Mom died, he didn't bring a single woman home. For a long time, I thought he was asexual or gay.'

They both laughed. After a while, Raj said again, 'Now you're worrying me. You guys won't get into a fight, right?'

'Arrrreyy, don't worry—just chill, I'll show you the place where I first had sex with a plumber!'

Raj laughed, not because of the possibility of visiting the site of Matt's chequered erotic life, but because he wanted Matt to continue saying arreys in this sweet manner, with extra Rs and extra stress on the Rs. Raj extended his left hand

and slid it between Matt's thighs. Matt said he was sure they were never going to reach Sioux Falls in one piece with so much distraction. Raj hoped Matt wasn't too anxious about meeting his father, about introducing his homophobic father to his brown husband. He didn't want to think about the break he wanted from the relationship. He wanted to think about the prospect of making love to Matt in the house where he had grown up.

*

Raj disliked Tony immediately, and it wasn't because he was a large man who welcomed them with a massive can of beer in his right hand. It wasn't because, as Matt had warned, Fox News was playing on the huge fifty-five-inch wall-mounted TV so loud that it was like walking into a movie theatre several minutes after the film had started. It wasn't even the fact that Tony had treated Matt badly once upon a time. Raj couldn't put his finger on what exactly it was about the man that put him off. But he didn't let his dislike show. He smiled at Tony, and Tony smiled back at him. Matt didn't hug his father, didn't shake his hands. He entered the house with a trying-hard-to-be-enthusiastic 'Hey Dad' and a smile that was exactly like the smile Tony had flashed at Raj, the kind of smile that indicates someone is in pain, or constipated. Raj greeted the smiling lady who came up to them, her earrings swaying vigorously.

'This is Irene,' Tony said.

'Hello, Irene,' Raj said.

Tony added in an enthusiastic voice, 'She's been cooking all day. She learned some new recipes from girlfriends at her church. It's all burgers and chicken and steak, and some salad, though. No kaboobs for Raj, sorry.'

Raj smiled. He didn't point out that they are kebabs not kaboobs, and was grateful the option of Indian food was considered to make him feel comfortable. 'That's alright, it sounds delicious.' Then after a pause, because he thought Tony and Irene would appreciate it, he added, 'I'm very excited.'

Matt gave him a strange look and Raj knew why—he wasn't the kind of person who liberally sprinkled his sentences with 'amazing', 'excited' and 'cool'. In fact, he often cribbed about the American tendency to use those words. He ignored Matt's puzzled look and tried not to laugh, and continued to wonder why he wasn't able to like Tony. Was it because of the Fox News that made it almost impossible for them to have a conversation? Irene suggested that they turn it off and Tony reluctantly agreed, only to switch it back on and play it on mute. I should be able to accept Tony as he is; I was, after all, warned adequately, Raj thought.

'I've always wanted to visit India, you know—my church made a trip to Calcutta last year,' Irene said during dinner. 'I'm sure it's a beautiful country.'

She had a singsong manner of speaking that Raj found both irritating and amusing. Raj didn't want to disappoint her by telling the truth—that most big cities in India were dustbowls and so overpopulated that it had almost turned him into a misanthrope.

He said instead, 'In parts, yes, it is beautiful. And it is a very large country. You won't find the cities beautiful, I am sure.' He paused, and then added without really meaning it, 'You must come. I would love to show you around.

Matt gave him that same look again.

'Maybe Tony and I could go for our honeymoon to see the Taj Mahal,' she said, rubbing Tony's hands, her voice now thin, high-pitched. Raj was a little annoyed because she wasn't pronouncing Taj Mahal properly. With the extra stress on the N, she wasn't even saying India properly.

Tony had a loud voice and sounded as if he was suffering from a cold. 'We'll see. I'm not sure, we will have to apply for visas and all. Are there lots of Muslims in India? I've heard there are.'

Matt and Raj exchanged glances. Raj wasn't offended, but he knew Matt would get angry. He was the kind of person who wore his liberalism on his sleeve and suffered from what Raj referred to as 'liberal guilt'. Raj had often asked him to get over it. In fact, when they first met, Raj had called him a 'Political Bottom', and Matt had paused for a bit and then said that 'only a super cute guy like you could get away with calling someone that'. Even after they began dating in earnest, Raj often told him that while he does need to be aware of race, Matt couldn't keep apologising for being white in a country where race relations were fucked up.

For the moment, Raj decided to focus on the baked chicken and served himself some more of the tasty beans and broccoli salad. He wanted to eat light. After he had confessed to Matt about the blowjob affair, they hadn't made love and he felt like making love that day. Raj had heard numerous stories about that house—Matt's fetish for hooking up with blue-collar straight or straight-acting workers, and how his English Setter dog would often bark relentlessly at the man who fucked Matt. It was in this house that Raj wanted to make love to Matt.

During dinner, Tony gulped down litres of beer, some of it dribbling down his chin. He interrupted Irene all the time and dominated the entire conversation with talk about cars and healthcare and how the government was taking his money away through taxes and how lazy people who didn't work were rewarded with food stamps. These were things that bothered Matt, not Raj.

'So where are you guys staying tonight?' Tony asked Matt, digging into his bowl of apple crumble topped with whipped cream.

Matt looked surprised. 'Oh, I thought we would just sleep in my room—is that okay?'

Raj wondered why Matt needed to add 'is that okay'. This was his house. The house he had grown up in. On their way in, after they had eaten at the restaurant by the freeway, Matt had spoken of how excited he was about sleeping on his own bed, in this house, after a long time. Raj wondered if 'is that okay' was a reflection of how hurt he was.

Raj braced himself for an altercation, an unpleasant situation where he would have to be in control in case Matt flipped. He looked at Irene who was so unsuspecting and so pleased with everything that it bored him. Eating slowly, he concentrated on the conversation, all set to defuse it, if required. Tony's civil (not warm, not loving) behaviour had given him the courage to do that. Otherwise, he had decided he would remain quiet most of the time and let the father and son speak.

Tony took a few seconds to think. 'No, it's fine. You can take your room. It's clean. Find the sheets in the storage bed.'

'Alright, thanks, Dad. You sure?'

'Yes, I just wasn't sure if you wanted to stay here. That's why I asked. You should always ask, right?'

Though he didn't look at Irene, or ask her, she said, 'Yes, how wonderful that you guys—'

As usual, he didn't let her finish and added that he would have asked the housekeeper to make the bed for them if Matt had told him earlier.

Raj spoke, with a tone of caution in his pace and voice, 'Tony, if it's a problem, we can book the American Inn, you know. It's just across the street.'

'Don't worry about it,' Tony said, looking at Raj. 'Stay here. You don't need to make that Patel any richer.' Matt thanked his Dad and paused for a few heavy moments, adding that Mr Patel was a very hard worker. Tony didn't respond to that. Instead, he asked Matt if he would join him outside for a smoke.

In the kitchen, Raj rinsed the dishes and placed them in the dishwasher, and Irene protested repeatedly. She said he was a sweetie. Though he was chatting with her, telling her how he had met Matt for the first time at a gay bar in Minneapolis, all he could think about was Matt's body, feeling hornier, and more conscious of his erection in front of Irene. He didn't dare check if it was showing, and he couldn't stop smiling at the possibility of passionate lovemaking in the same bed that Matt had grown up sleeping in. That bed magnified the importance of the act for him—as if it would somehow make him a part of Matt's childhood, part of the special experience of the man he loved. Then, the thought of taking a break returned, and he turned soft and felt drained of energy. It would be difficult to broach the topic with Matt. Suddenly, Raj realised: three days ago, it was just a thought, and now it had almost morphed into a decision.

Raj thought of the times he and Matt had travelled together, the way airport security would often take Raj aside to check his hands for gunpowder residue and Matt hovered nearby, talking, sometimes even trying to hold Raj's hands. Though they never talked about it, it was understood that Matt would remain close by at every domestic airport.

When they travelled to India, Raj's nervousness about travel vanished like camphor blending with air—as if the moment he stepped into the Air India fight, he became a full person: less vigilant, less careful, less apologetic. In the US, when he wasn't frisked by TSA, wasn't stopped and asked questions, he felt smaller and smaller, as if he wasn't a whole person, as if he needed Matt to make him whole, validate his existence as a real human. Matt's calm after the cheating incident made him cringe: why did he always need to be so good? Why did he have to be so righteous? If they took a break, Raj would be on his own, out from under Matt's suffocating protection. The dishwasher was now making familiar sounds of water mixing with soap and water splashing on the dishes.

'I hope they don't end up having an argument,' Irene said, mopping the granite kitchen slab with an orange cotton dishcloth and asking him if he would like some coffee. 'I bought some really good coffee.'

'Oh, I won't mind some coffee. Thanks, Irene.'

'Do you think they'll argue?' Irene asked, looking a bit anxious. 'Don't worry, Irene, I think they both just want to forget the past. They are sort of determined to wave the white fag.'

Irene chuckled, 'That's a nice way to put it.' Though she chuckled, she sounded nervous and added that she was a little worried about Tony.

Raj asked if he said something to her.

'No, I mean—I am sure Matt knooows this,' she said looking straight into his eyes in a way that meant she was saying something extremely obvious. 'Tony gets a bit anxious when there are guests. Every time you went to use the restroom, he kept asking where you were, wanted us to go and check on you. He just likes to be in—you know—full control. It took him a while to let me stay over, too.'

'Relationships are complicated.'

'I agree, but not always—look at YOU TWO,' she said cheerfully, loudly, rubbing her hands together. Raj wondered if she was nervous. 'But you're right,' she added in a matter of-fact tone with a shrug, 'relationships are complicated. My son hasn't seen me in six years. I don't even know if he's okay.

Raj asked, 'Why? I'm sorry—I don't mean to pry, but that's a little upsetting.' He paused before saying the words 'little upsetting' and between little and upsetting he paused again—a breath or two.

She now burst out into a shy giggle. Then she came closer, flung the towel on to the kitchen slab, and whispered, 'I slapped his wife.'

'Oh my god … you don't look like the slapping kind!' Raj was laughing now.

'Oh yes, I can do that. She called me a bitch. And I said, you want to know what a real bitch looks like? Take this!'

And when both of them burst into a loud laughter, Matt and Tony joined them in the kitchen, but it didn't stop them from laughing. In between the laughter, Irene told Tony that she'd told Raj about slapping her daughter-in-law, and Tony said 'Oh that was intense,' and grumbled that only a stupid bitch would call a lovely woman like Irene a bitch.

*

Raj and Matt kissed each other passionately, first on the couch, and then while climbing up the stairs. Matt sat down on the carpeted stairs and let Raj nibble on his chest, around his neck, grab his ass. 'We should go up,' he mumbled and Raj said that he couldn't wait to, but Matt would have to show the way because Raj didn't know the house. They sort of crawled up the stairs, rolled on the carpeted floor and entered a room that Matt pushed open with one hand while he kept his other hand busy between Raj's legs. It was a medium-sized room; dark, with enough light streaming in from the street to show them the window, the queen-sized bed, the table with a lamp that Matt extended a hand to switch on. There was now enough light for them to navigate the room even through the passionate intimacy without stumbling into or colliding with anything.

'Do you want to find fresh sheets,' Raj asked as he was pulling up Matt's T-shirt, but Matt said he didn't care, his hands still inside Raj's zipper, caressing him into hardness. He picked up Raj and placed him gently on the bed. Against his bare buttocks, Raj felt something hard, sharp. Not sharp enough to cut through his skin, but sharp. As if he sat on a bed of pencils and twigs. And the thing creaked. In the dim light, as Matt went down on him, he turned around to look, screamed at the top of his voice and sprang up from the bed, knocking Matt's nose with a thud. When Matt switched on the lights, Raj was on the floor, leaning against the wall on the opposite side of the bed, shocked, breathing fast. Matt was holding his nose.

'Raj!' Matt rushed towards him. But Raj pushed him away, pointing to the bed, breathing fast and saying fuck fuck fuck, what the fuck is that? Then, the door flung open and Irene and Tony walked in, and saw Raj—shirtless, pants and briefs pulled to his thighs, with an erect penis, breathing fast, saying what the fuck is that. Raj wanted to die. Irene gasped and Tony screamed, 'What the—'

'Dad!' No one said a thing.

'Dad, what the hell is this? What's this doing here?' Matt asked, pained, pointing to the bed.

Raj was standing now, his pants back on his waist, his hands folded, face twisted in fear and disgust. 'I need some air, Matt.'

'Raj, please wait.'

'I'll see you downstairs. I'm sorry, I can't be in this room.'

He didn't say excuse me before Irene moved aside. He sat on the large couch downstairs, still panting, still embarrassed. The house was quiet and, from where he sat, he could hear them talking. Not bits and pieces, but all of it. Agitated voices.

'What do you mean, why did I do this? I did nothing!' Tony's voice.

'You did nothing? You did nothing? Then what is this? What is this nasty, dirty thing doing here on my bed? Shouldn't it be in the basement? How many hundreds of years old is it?'

'I did nothing.' Tony repeated.

'Dad please, you went upstairs after we smoked. What were you doing upstairs?'

'I was checking—' Irene started to complain, 'Honey, I have told you so many times to just throw these things away, but you just hoard them. I mean, you just hoard—'

'Oh, shut up, Irene.' Irene didn't stop speaking, 'How scared I was when I came across it one day. Oh god, that boy, he is scared, such a sweetie he is.'

'It's fake—just a Halloween thing.' Tony's tone was dismissive. 'Your boyfriend is overreacting!'

Raj was breathing normally now. He was full of guilt and shame. He covered his face with his hands and tried to recollect what had just happened. More than his fear at discovering the skull, he was ashamed that two new people had discovered him in that state: helpless, panting, his pants down; he couldn't bear to face them anymore. It would be a little cold outside, not much. He put on a jacket, his socks, his shoes, his red silk scarf. He took out his smartphone and confirmed whether the hotel across the street was open.

'Raj!' Matt was coming down the stairs. 'Raj, where are you?'

Tony screamed behind him, 'Hey, I told you that the room hadn't been used in a while.'

Raj gathered his suitcase. He was calm, a bit too calm, when he spoke. He didn't raise his voice. He wasn't agitated. He apologised for waking them up so late and for freaking out about the fake skeleton, and said that it had looked so real when he first saw it in the hazy light, and that he was a bit tired, and would rather book a room at the American Inn.

'Oh,' Tony said.

'Oh,' Irene added. 'Are you sure, sweetie?'

'Yes, please don't worry. I'll see you all for breakfast, or maybe you guys can join me there.'

It was Matt who screamed, it was Matt who lost his temper, 'What do you mean join you for breakfast?'

'Matt! Stop screaming.' Raj was cold and calm. 'It's fine. You stay here. I'll see you in the morning.'

'I'm coming with you.'

It was cold outside. Matt followed Raj, who walked out without any further words. The road was empty and quiet. There was no wind but it was cold still. The cold nights of fall that hid the multi-coloured leaves.

He turned around and looked at Matt and almost whispered, 'You want to work things out with your father. You stay.

Afterwards, in the hotel room, holding the free coffee that he poured himself at the reception of (hardworking, rich) Mr Patel's American Inn, he wondered what Matt might be doing. Was he arguing with his father? Was he sitting in one corner and still figuring out what just happened? It always took a while for Matt to figure out such things. He would go for a smoke and think. Now, holding the free coffee, in Mr Patel's American Inn, Raj wondered what there was to figure out, why he would need more time before he stormed out of the house. Raj decided he had overreacted. He'd been scared, but if Irene hadn't seen him half-naked, if Tony hadn't seen his erect penis, maybe he would have stayed. Or maybe he wouldn't have.

But it was over now. As soon as Matt gave him that puzzled expression outside the house, in that nippy fall night, he knew it was over between them. He switched on the TV and changed channels until he found CNN.

Raj realised he didn't like Tony on sight because he looked so like Matt, they were almost carbon copies. He was worried Matt would grow old to look like that, the list of things that drove him nuts would grow longer and longer, and he would always justify everything with his Larger Picture Theory. And in that tattered and old carbon copy of a face that was so uncomfortable to have Raj in the house, he saw an aged, unhappy, frustrated and frightened Matt. There was a knock on the door an hour later.

'I'm sorry,' Matt said.

Raj felt something snap inside his chest, like an artery or something. He wept and said that, no, he was sorry. He added that he should have stayed back; a bond with his father was important for Matt. Raj said he was sorry that he overreacted.

'You shouldn't be apologising; he did it. He put it there on purpose.'

'It doesn't matter, Matt. I am so glad you are here. I thought—' Matt stopped him, held his hand. 'Don't go there.'

He unzipped his duffel bag and took out a fresh towel— he didn't like using towels in hotels. Then he spoke in a low, regretful voice, 'You know what? I screamed at him.'

'Oh.' Raj gasped and covered his face. 'I am so sorry, I shouldn't have reacted like that. This is all my fault.'

'Raj! Don't say that. I would have probably had a heart attack if I saw that skeleton. And I didn't scream at him for putting it there because there was no way I could have proven that. I screamed at him because ...' Matt paused and looked away. 'You might find this odd, but I was ready to stay there for another couple of hours and talk to him, teach him tolerance. But he kept saying "your boyfriend" when he talked about you. Your boyfriend is overreacting, your boyfriend shouldn't have left like that, and I couldn't take it anymore. I screamed at him. I said, Dad, he is my husband, I married him, I took vows to live with him forever, he isn't my boyfriend.'

Raj hugged Matt so tight that he may well have broken bones. He didn't want to think about the break that he wanted to take even a few hours ago; he didn't want to think about whether he would have wanted to grow old with Matt if he had turned up in the morning.